I0818447

RIVER OF BONES

AND OTHER STORIES

ALSO BY REBECCA ROANHORSE

BETWEEN EARTH AND SKY

Black Sun
Fevered Star
Mirrored Heavens

THE SIXTH WORLD

Trail of Lightning
Storm of Locusts

Star Wars: Resistance Reborn
Race to the Sun
Tread of Angels

RIVER OF BONES

AND OTHER STORIES

REBECCA ROANHORSE

LONDON NEW YORK TORONTO
AMSTERDAM/ANTWERP NEW DELHI SYDNEY/MELBOURNE

1230 AVENUE OF THE AMERICAS, NEW YORK, NEW YORK 10020

This book is a work of fiction. Any references to historical events, real people, or real places are used fictitiously. Other names, characters, places, and events are products of the author's imagination, and any resemblance to actual events or places or persons, living or dead, is entirely coincidental.

The stories in this collection first appeared in the following magazines and anthologies: "Welcome to Your Authentic Indian Experience™" in *Apex Magazine* (August 2017); "Harvest" in *New Suns: Original Speculative Fiction by People of Color,* edited by Nisi Shawl; "Wherein Abigail Fields Recalls Her First Death, and, Subsequently, Her Best Life" in *A Phoenix First Must Burn: Sixteen Stories of Black Girl Magic, Resistance, and Hope,* edited by Patrice Caldwell; "The Boys from Blood River" in *Vampires Never Get Old: Tales with Fresh Bite,* edited by Zoraida Córdova and Natalie C. Parker; "White Hills" in *Never Whistle at Night: An Indigenous Dark Fiction Anthology,* edited by Shane Hawk and Theodore C. Van Alst Jr.; "A Brief Lesson in Native American Astronomy" in *The Mythic Dream,* edited by Dominik Parisien and Navah Wolfe; "Falling Bodies" published by Amazon Original Stories; and "Eye & Tooth" in *Out There Screaming,* edited by Jordan Peele.

First Saga Press hardcover edition March 2026

SAGA PRESS and colophon are trademarks of Simon & Schuster, LLC

Interior design by Lewelin Polanco

Manufactured in the United States of America

1 3 5 7 9 10 8 6 4 2

Library of Congress Control Number has been applied for.

ISBN 978-1-9821-5381-6

ISBN 978-1-9821-5383-0 (ebook)

To Juanita

Who taught me to love stories

CONTENTS

INTRODUCTION

This collection is the culmination of the first eight years of my writing career. It includes the very first story I ever wrote and published, "Welcome to Your Authentic Indian Experience™," and ends with "River of Bones," a novella set in a climate-apocalyptic Southwest created in my first novel. It is a fitting closure to this phase of my writing life—a journey I never expected to go on, nor could I have foreseen where it would take me.

Short stories, more than anything, are a snapshot of an author in a particular time and place, and the stories collected here are no exception. Authors, like all people, grow and change throughout the years, and while certain themes may recur throughout a body of work, the person writing the story, if they are lucky, is not the same person they were a decade ago. I sometimes think of the person I was when I started and who I am today and wonder if these past and present iterations of myself would recognize each other. Probably not.

So, along with you, reader, I am rediscovering some of these stories, and through them, rediscovering myself. It's not always comfortable, but it is certainly interesting.

"Welcome to Your Authentic Indian Experience™" has proven to be my most enduring story. It has been translated into dozens of languages and republished in everything from fanzines to technology ethics textbooks. It won the Hugo and Nebula Awards and was a finalist for the Sturgeon, Locus, and World Fantasy Awards. It is the story of a man trying to live up to the image of who he thinks the world wants him to be only to realize the illusion is much more desirable than the real thing. While it is specifically about Native identity and displacement, its popularity tells me that it resonates with marginalized people of various backgrounds. We are all striving to be what the world tells us we should be. "Welcome to Your Authentic Indian Experience™" asks, at what cost.

"A Harvest of Beating Hearts" was a Parallax Award honoree. It is a story about desire and how obsession can drive us to darkness. There is horror here, but also beauty. There is unspeakable violence against the innocent, but also justice. Or is that simply revenge? What do we owe history? What do we owe our ancestors? What do we owe ourselves?

There is not a lot of fiction that explores the life of Black women in the American Southwest, and "Wherein Abigail Fields Recalls Her First Death, and, Subsequently, Her Best Life" gave me the chance to do that in a fantasy setting. Originally a submission for a Young Adult anthology celebrating Black Girl Magic called *A Phoenix First Must Burn* (a phrase coined by pioneering Black speculative fiction writer Octavia Butler) I wanted to tell the story of a girl who has to die to rise and, once unburdened, is free to love as she wishes.

There is a stretch of Highway 287 from Amarillo to Fort Worth, TX, that winds through a series of small towns that feel left behind by the modern world. (Less so now, but I've been driving that road for forty years and a lot has changed.) "The Boys from Blood River" is set in a fictional version of one of those towns. Driving through, I would often glimpse the old high school, usually the grandest building around, and wonder what poor teenager was stuck in this roadside speed trap. Worse, what if they were brown or queer or both. And what if a beautiful cowboy rolled into town and offered them a way out? All they had to do was become a killer.

"White Hills" is one of my personal favorites and the one that gets the most extreme reactions. It is very much a IYKYK story about assimilation and the very narrow space where respectability politics lives and dies.

"A Brief Lesson in Native American Astronomy" won the Ignyte Award and was a Locus Award finalist and a Kindred Award honoree. It is a retelling of a Tewa story. I originally wrote it for an anthology about mythic retellings. I could have gone with something more traditional, like a Greek or Nordic myth, but the warnings about vanity, obsession, and fame seemed particularly resonant for our times.

While I write about identity quite frequently, I had never written about being a transracial adoptee until "Falling Bodies." It is definitely the hot stove of my identity, too dangerous to touch for very long, but I tried to capture some of the deep, conflicting emotions of being a transracial adoptee and the very real desperation to escape, at all costs, the narratives thrust upon you by the people who are meant to love you the best. It was a Eugie Foster Memorial Award finalist and the recipient of the Summit Award.

"Eye & Tooth" was written for Jordan Peele's Black Horror anthology. I wanted to show up for Black people in Texas, hunt some monsters, and have fun. As for monsters making the best monster hunters, we all know game recognizes game.

As for "River of Bones"? That one is for the fans. I have received hundreds of emails, DMs, and in-person requests asking me when I would return to Maggie and Kai, the protagonists of my first novel. The truth is that I thought I had closed that chapter of my creative journey, but when my editor asked me to consider revisiting the Sixth World to give the story some closure, I couldn't say no. I also very much wanted to visit the Burque (a post-apocalyptic Albuquerque), even if only briefly.

Thank you all for going on this journey with me. Hopefully, there is something in this collection that you love, and maybe something you hate, but that at least makes you think. Maybe you see yourself in these stories, or maybe you only seek to understand someone else a little better for a few moments in time . . . at least before they change into someone else. Identity is fluid, desire kills, and survival makes one a monster.

WELCOME TO YOUR AUTHENTIC INDIAN EXPERIENCE™

In the Great American Indian novel, when it is finally written, all of the white people will be Indians and all of the Indians will be ghosts.

—SHERMAN ALEXIE, "HOW TO WRITE THE GREAT AMERICAN INDIAN NOVEL"

You maintain a menu of a half dozen Experiences on your digital blackboard, but Vision Quest is the one the Tourists choose the most. That certainly makes your workday easy. All a Vision Quest requires is a dash of mystical shaman, a spirit animal (wolf usually, but birds of prey are on the upswing this year), and the approximation of a peyote experience. Tourists always come out of the Experience feeling spiritually transformed. (You've never actually tried peyote, but you did smoke your share of weed during that one year at Arizona State, and who's going to call you on the difference?) It's all 101 stuff, really, these Quests. But no other Indian working at Sedona Sweats can do it better. Your sales numbers are tops.

Your wife Theresa doesn't approve of the gig. Oh, she likes you working, especially after that dismal stretch of unemployment the year before last when she almost left you, but she thinks the job itself is demeaning.

"Our last name's not Trueblood," she complains when you tell her about your *nom de rêve*.

"Nobody wants to buy a Vision Quest from a Jesse Turnblatt," you explain. "I need to sound more Indian."

"You are Indian," she says. "Turnblatt's Indian-sounding enough because you're already Indian."

"We're not the right kind of Indian," you counter. "I mean, we're Catholic, for Christ's sake."

What Theresa doesn't understand is that Tourists don't want a real Indian experience. They want what they see in the movies, and who can blame them? Movie Indians are terrific! So you watch the same movies the Tourists do, until John Dunbar becomes your spirit animal and Stands with a Fist your best girl. You memorize Johnny Depp's lines from *The Lone Ranger* and hang a picture of Iron Eyes Cody in your work locker. For a while you are really into Dustin Hoffman's *Little Big Man*.

It's *Little Big Man* that does you in.

For a week in June, you convince your boss to offer a Custer's Last Stand special, thinking there might be a Tourist or two who want to live out a Crazy Horse Experience. You even memorize some quotes attributed to the venerable Sioux chief that you find on the internet. You plan to make it real authentic.

But you don't get a single taker. Your numbers nosedive.

Management in Phoenix notices, and Boss drops it from the blackboard by Fourth of July weekend. He yells at you to stop screwing around, accuses you of trying to be an artiste or whatnot.

"Tourists don't come to Sedona Sweats to live out a goddamn battle," Boss says in the break room over lunch one day, "especially if the white guy loses. They come here to find themselves." Boss waves his hand in the air in an approximation of something vaguely prayer-like. "It's a spiritual experience we're offering. Top quality. The fucking best."

DarAnne, your Navajo coworker with the pretty smile and the perfect teeth, snorts loudly. She takes a bite of her sandwich, mutton by the looks of it. Her jaw works, her sharp teeth flash white. She waits until she's finished chewing to say, "Nothing spiritual about Squaw Fantasy."

Squaw Fantasy is Boss's latest idea, his way to get the numbers up and impress Management. DarAnne and a few others have complained about the use of the ugly slur, the inclusion of a sexual fantasy as an Experience at all. But Boss is unmoved, especially when the first week's numbers roll in. Biggest seller yet.

Boss looks over at you. "What do you think?"

Boss is Pima, with a bushy mustache and a thick head of still-dark hair. You admire that about him. Virility. Boss makes being a man look easy. Makes everything look easy. Real authentic-like.

DarAnne tilts her head, long beaded earrings swinging, and waits. Her painted nails click impatiently against the Formica lunch table. You can smell the onion in her sandwich.

Your mouth is dry like the red rock desert you can see outside your window. If you say Squaw Fantasy is demeaning, Boss will mock you, call you a pussy, or worse. If you say you think it's okay, DarAnne and her crew will put you on the guys-who-are-assholes list and you'll deserve it.

You sip your bottled water, stalling. Decide that in the wake of the Crazy Horse debacle that Boss's approval means more than DarAnne's and venture, "I mean, if the Tourists like it . . ."

Boss slaps the table, triumphant. DarAnne's face twists in disgust. "What does Theresa think of that, eh, Jesse?" she spits at you. "You tell her Boss is thinking of adding Savage Braves to the menu next? He's gonna have you in a loincloth and hair down to your ass, see how you like it."

Your face heats up, embarrassed. You push away from the table, too quickly, and the flimsy top teeters. You can hear Boss's shouts of protest as his vending machine lemonade tilts dangerously, and DarAnne's mocking laugh, but it all comes to your ears through a shroud of thick cotton. You mumble something about getting back to work. The sound of arguing trails you down the hall.

You change in the locker room and shuffle down to the pod marked with your name. You unlock the hatch and crawl in. Some people find the pods claustrophobic, but you like the cool metal container, the tight fit. It's comforting. The VR helmet fits snugly on your head, the breathing mask over your nose and mouth.

With a shiver of anticipation, you give the pod your Experience setting. Add the other necessary details to flesh things out. The screen prompts you to pick a Tourist connection from a waiting list, but you ignore it, blinking through the option screens until you get to the final confirmation. You brace for the mild nausea that always comes when you Relocate in and out of an Experience.

The first sensation is always smell. Sweetgrass and woodsmoke and the rich loam of the northern plains. Even though it's fake, receptors firing under the coaxing of a machine, you relax into the scents. You grew up in the desert, among people who appreciate cedar and piñon and red earth, but there's still something homelike about this prairie place.

Or maybe you watch too much TV. You really aren't sure anymore.

You find yourself on a wide grassy plain, somewhere in the upper Midwest of a bygone era. Bison roam in the distance. A hawk soars overhead.

You are alone, you know this, but it doesn't stop you from looking around to make sure. This thing you are about to do. Well, you would be humiliated if anyone found out. Because you keep thinking about what DarAnne said. Squaw Fantasy and Savage Braves. Because the thing is, being sexy doesn't disgust you the way it does DarAnne. You've never been one of those guys. The star athlete or the cool kid. It's tempting to think of all those Tourist women wanting you like that, even if it is just in an Experience.

You are now wearing a knee-length loincloth. A wave of black hair flows down your back. Your middle-aged paunch melts into rock-hard abs worthy of a romance novel cover model. You raise your chin and try out your best stoic look on a passing prairie dog. The little rodent chirps something back at you. You've heard prairie dogs can remember human faces, and you wonder what this one would say about you. Then you remember this is an Experience, so the prairie dog is no more real than the caricature of an Indian you have conjured up.

You wonder what Theresa would think if she saw you like this.

The world shivers. The pod screen blinks on. Someone wants your Experience.

A Tourist, asking for you. Completely normal. Expected. No need for that panicky hot breath rattling through your mask.

You scroll through the Tourist's requirements.

Experience Type: Vision Quest.

Tribe: Plains Indian (nation nonspecific).

Favorite Animal: Wolf.

These things are all familiar. Things you are good at faking. Things you get paid to pretend.

You drop the Savage Brave fantasy garb for buckskin pants and beaded leather moccasins. You keep your chest bare and muscled, but you drape a rough wool blanket across your shoulders for dignity. Your impressive abs are still visible.

The sun is setting and you turn to put the artificial dusk at your back, prepared to meet your Tourist. You run through your list of Indian names to bestow upon your Tourist once the Vision Quest is over. You like to keep the names fresh, never using the same one in case the Tourists ever compare notes. For a while you cheated and used one of those naming things on the internet where you enter your favorite flower and the street you grew up on and it gives you your Indian name, but there were too many Tourists who grew up on Elm or Park and you found yourself getting repetitive. You try to base the names on appearances now. Hair color, eye color, some distinguishing feature. Tourists really seem to like it.

This Tourist is younger than you expected. Sedona Sweats caters to New Agers, the kind from Los Angeles or Scottsdale with impressive bank accounts. But the man coming up the hill, squinting into the setting sun, is in his late twenties. Medium height and build with pale, spotty skin and brown hair. The guy looks normal enough, but there's something sad about him.

Maybe he's lost.

You imagine a lot of Tourists are lost.

Maybe he's someone who works a day job just like you, saving up money for this once-in-a-lifetime Indian Experience™. Maybe he's desperate, looking for purpose in his own shitty world and thinking Indians have all the answers. Maybe he just wants something that's authentic.

You like that. The idea that Tourists come to you to experience something real. DarAnne has it wrong. The Tourists aren't all bad. They're just needy.

You plant your feet in a wide welcoming stance and raise one hand. "How," you intone, as the man stops a few feet in front of you.

The man flushes, a bright pinkish tone. You can't tell if he's nervous or embarrassed. Maybe both? But he raises his hand, palm forward, and says "How" right back.

"Have you come seeking wisdom, my son?" you ask in your best broken English accent. "Come. I will show you great wisdom." You sweep your arm across the prairie. "We look to brother wolf—"

The man rolls his eyes.

What?

You stutter to a pause. Are you doing something wrong? Is the accent no good? Too little? Too much?

You visualize the requirements checklist. You are positive he chose wolf. Positive. So you press on. "My brother wolf," you say again, this time sounding much more Indian, you are sure.

"I'm sorry," the man says, interrupting. "This wasn't what I wanted. I've made a mistake."

"But you picked it on the menu!" In the confusion of the moment, you drop your accent. Is it too late to go back and say it right?

The man's lips curl up in a grimace, like you have confirmed his worst suspicions. He shakes his head. "I was looking for something more authentic."

Something in your chest seizes up.

"I can fix it," you say.

"No, it's all right. I'll find someone else." He turns to go.

You can't afford another bad mark on your record. No more screwups or you're out. Boss made that clear enough. "At least give me a chance," you plead.

"It's okay," he says over his shoulder.

This is bad. Does this man not know what a good Indian you are? "Please!"

The man turns back to you, his face thoughtful.

You feel a surge of hope. This can be fixed, and you know exactly how. "I can give you a name. Something you can call yourself when you need to feel strong. It's authentic," you add enthusiastically. "From a real Indian." That much is true.

The man looks a little more open, and he doesn't say no. That's good enough.

You study the man's dusky hair, his pinkish skin. His long skinny legs. He reminds you a bit of the flamingos at the Albuquerque zoo, but you are pretty sure no one wants to be named after those strange creatures. It must be something good. Something . . . spiritual.

"Your name is Pale Crow," you offer. Birds are still on your mind.

At the look on the man's face, you reconsider. "No, no, it is White"—yes, that's better than pale—"Wolf. White Wolf."

"White Wolf?" There's a note of interest in his voice.

You nod sagely. You knew the man had picked wolf. Your eyes meet. Uncomfortably. White Wolf coughs into his hand. "I really should be getting back."

"But you paid for the whole Experience. Are you sure?"

White Wolf is already walking away.

"But . . ."

You feel the exact moment he Relocates out of the Experience.

A sensation like part of your soul is being stretched too thin. Then, a sort of whiplash as you let go.

The Hey U.S.A. bar is the only Indian bar in Sedona. The basement level of a driftwood-paneled strip mall across the street from work. It's packed with the after-shift crowd, most of them pod jockeys like you, but also a few roadside jewelry hawkers and restaurant stiffs still smelling like frybread grease. You're lucky to find a spot at the far end next to the servers' station. You slip onto the plastic-covered barstool and raise a hand to get the bartender's attention.

"So what do you really think?" asks a voice to your right. DarAnne is staring at you, her eyes accusing and her posture tense.

This is it. A second chance. Your opportunity to stay off the assholes list. You need to get this right. You try to think of something clever to say, something that would impress her but let you save face, too. But you've never been all that clever, so you stick to the truth.

"I think I really need this job," you admit.

DarAnne's shoulders relax.

"Scooch over," she says to the man on the other side of her, and he obligingly shifts off his stool to let her sit. "I knew it," she says. "Why didn't you stick up for me? Why are you so afraid of Boss?"

"I'm not afraid of Boss. I'm afraid of Theresa leaving me. And unemployment."

"You gotta get a backbone, Jesse, is all."

You realize the bartender is waiting, impatient. You drink the same thing every time you come here, a single Coors Light in a cold bottle. But the bartender never remembers you, or your order. You turn to offer to buy one for DarAnne, but she's already gone, back with her crew.

You drink your beer alone, wait a reasonable amount of time, and leave.

White Wolf is waiting for you under the streetlight at the corner.

The bright neon Indian Chief that squats atop Sedona Sweats hovers behind him in pinks and blues and yellows, his huge hand blinking up and down in greeting. White puffs of smoke signals flicker up, up, and away beyond his far shoulder.

You don't recognize White Wolf at first. Most people change themselves a little within the construct of the Experience. Nothing wrong with being thinner, taller, a little better looking. But White Wolf looks exactly the same. Nondescript brown hair, pale skin, long legs.

"How." White Wolf raises his hand, unconsciously mimicking the big neon Chief. At least he has the decency to look embarrassed when he does it.

"You." You are so surprised that the accusation is the first thing out of your mouth. "How did you find me?"

"Trueblood, right? I asked around."

"And people told you?" This is very against the rules.

"I asked who the best Spirit Guide was. If I was going to buy a Vision Quest, who should I go to. Everyone said you."

You flush, feeling vindicated, but also annoyed that your co-workers had given your name out to a Tourist. "I tried to tell you," you say ungraciously.

"I should have listened." White Wolf smiles, a faint shifting of his mouth into something like contrition. An awkward pause ensues.

"We're really not supposed to fraternize," you finally say.

"I know, I just . . . I just wanted to apologize. For ruining the Experience like that."

"It's no big deal," you say, gracious this time. "You paid, right?"

"Yeah."

"It's just . . ." You know this is your ego talking, but you need to know. "Did I do something wrong?"

"No, it was me. You were great. It's just, I had a great-grandmother who was Cherokee, and I think being there, seeing everything. Well, it really stirred something in me. Like, ancestral memory or something."

You've heard of ancestral memories, but you've also heard of people claiming Cherokee blood where there is none. Theresa calls them "pretendians," but you think that's unkind. Maybe White Wolf really is Cherokee. You don't know any Cherokees, so maybe they really do look like this guy. There's a half-Tlingit in payroll and he's pale.

"Well, I've got to get home," you say. "My wife, and all."

White Wolf nods. "Sure, sure. I just. Thank you."

"For what?"

But White Wolf's already walking away. "See you around."

A little déjà vu shudders your bones, but you chalk it up to Tourists. Who understands them, anyway?

You go home to Theresa.

As soon as you slide into your pod the next day, your monitor lights up. There's already a Tourist on deck and waiting.

"Shit," you mutter, pulling up the menu and scrolling quickly through the requirements. Everything looks good, good, except . . . a sliver of panic when you see that a specific tribe has been requested. Cherokee. You don't know anything about Cherokees. What they wore back then, their ceremonies. The only Cherokee you know is . . .

White Wolf shimmers into your Experience.

In your haste, you have forgotten to put on your buckskin. Your Experience-self still wears Wranglers and Nikes. Boss would be pissed to see you this sloppy.

"Why are you back?" you ask.

"I thought maybe we could just talk."

"About what?"

White Wolf shrugs. "Doesn't matter. Whatever."

"I can't."

"Why not? This is my time. I'm paying."

You feel a little panicked. A Tourist has never broken protocol like this before. Part of why the Experience works is that everyone knows their role. But White Wolf don't seem to care about the rules.

"I can just keep coming back," he says. "I have money, you know."

"You'll get me in trouble."

"I won't. I just . . ." White Wolf hesitates. Something in him slumps. What you read as arrogance now looks like desperation. "I need a friend."

You know that feeling. The truth is, you could use a friend, too. Someone to talk to. What could the harm be? You'll just be two men, talking.

Not here, though. You still need to work. "How about the bar?"

"The place from last night?"

"I get off at eleven."

When you get there around 11:30, the bar is busy but you recognize White Wolf immediately. A skinny white guy stands out at the Hey U.S.A. It's funny. Under this light, in this crowd, White Wolf could pass for Native of some kind. One of those 1⁄64th guys, at least. Maybe he really is a little Cherokee from way back when.

White Wolf waves you over to an empty booth. A Coors Light waits for you. You slide into the booth and wrap a hand around the cool, damp skin of the bottle, pleasantly surprised.

"A lucky guess, did I get it right?"

You nod and take a sip. That first sip is always magic. Like how you imagine Golden, Colorado, must feel like on a winter morning.

"So," White Wolf says, "tell me about yourself."

You look around the bar for familiar faces. Are you really going to do this? Tell a Tourist about your life? Your real life? A little voice in your head whispers that maybe this isn't so smart. Boss could find out and get mad. DarAnne could make fun of you. Besides, White Wolf will want a cool story, something real authentic, and all you have is an aging three-bedroom ranch and a student loan.

But he's looking at you, friendly interest, and nobody looks at you like that much anymore, not even Theresa. So you talk.

Not everything.

But some. Enough.

Enough that when the bartender calls last call, you realize you've been talking for two hours.

When you stand up to go, White Wolf stands up, too. You shake hands, Indian-style, which makes you smile. You didn't expect it, but you've got a good, good feeling.

"So, same time tomorrow?" White Wolf asks.

You're tempted, but, "No, Theresa will kill me if I stay out this late two nights in a row." And then, "But how about Friday?"

"Friday it is." White Wolf touches your shoulder. "See you then, Jesse."

You feel a warm flutter of anticipation for Friday. "See you."

—

Friday you are there by 11:05. White Wolf laughs when he sees your face, and you grin back, only a little embarrassed. This time you pay for the drinks, and the two of you pick up right where you left off. It's so easy. White Wolf never seems to tire of your stories, and it's been so long since you had a new friend to tell them to that you can't seem to quit. It turns out White Wolf loves Kevin Costner, too, and you take turns quoting lines at each other until White Wolf stumps you with a Wind in His Hair quote.

"Are you sure that's in the movie?"

"It's Lakota!"

You won't admit it, but you're impressed with how good White Wolf's Lakota sounds.

White Wolf smiles. "Looks like I know something you don't."

You wave it away good-naturedly, but vow to watch the movie again.

Time flies and once again, after last call, you both stand outside under the Big Chief. You happily agree to meet again next Tuesday. And the following Friday. Until it becomes your new routine.

The month passes quickly. The next month too.

"You seem too happy," Theresa says one night, sounding suspicious.

You grin and wrap your arms around your wife, pulling her close until her rose-scented shampoo fills your nose. "Just made a friend, is all. A guy from work." You decide to keep it vague. Hanging with White Wolf, who you've long stopped thinking of as just a Tourist, would be hard to explain.

"You're not stepping out on me, Jesse Turnblatt? Because I will—"

You cut her off with a kiss. "Are you jealous?"

"Should I be?"

"Never."

She sniffs, but lets you kiss her again, her soft body tight against yours.

"I love you," you murmur as your hands dip under her shirt.

"You better."

Tuesday morning and you can't breathe. Your nose is a deluge of snot and your joints ache. Theresa calls in sick for you and bundles you in bed with a bowl of stew. You're supposed to meet White Wolf for your usual drink, but you're much too sick. You consider sending Theresa with a note but decide against it. It's only one night. White Wolf will understand.

But by Friday the coughing has become a deep rough bellow that shakes your whole chest. When Theresa calls in sick for you again, you make sure your cough is loud enough for Boss to hear it. Pray he doesn't dock you for the days you're missing. But what you're most worried about is standing up White Wolf again.

"Do you think you could go for me?" you ask Theresa.

"What, down to the bar? I don't drink."

"I'm not asking you to drink. Just to meet him, let him know I'm sick. He's probably thinking I forgot about him."

"Can't you call him?"

"I don't have his number."

"Fine, then. What's his name?"

You hesitate. Realize you don't know. The only name you know is the one you gave him. "White Wolf."

"Okay, then. Get some rest."

Theresa doesn't get back until almost one a.m. "Where were you?" you ask, alarmed. Is that a rosy flush in her cheeks, the scent of Cherry Coke on her breath?

"At the bar like you asked me to."

"What took so long?"

She huffs. "Did you want me to go or not?"

"Yes, but . . . well, did you see him?"

She nods, smiles a little smile that you've never seen on her before.

"What is it?" Something inside you shrinks.

"A nice man. Real nice. You didn't tell me he was Cherokee."

By Monday you're able to drag yourself back to work. There's a note taped to your locker to go see Boss. You find him in his office, looking through the reports he sends to Management every week.

"I hired a new guy."

You swallow the excuses you've prepared to explain how sick you were, your promises to get your numbers up. They become a hard ball in your throat.

"Sorry, Jesse." Boss actually does look a little sorry. "This guy is good, a real rez guy. Last name's Wolf. I mean, shit, you can't get more Indian than that. The Tourists are going to eat it up."

"The Tourists love me, too." You sound whiny, but you can't help it. There's a sinking feeling in your gut that tells you this is bad, bad, bad.

"You're good, Jesse. But nobody knows anything about Pueblo Indians, so all you've got is that TV shit. This guy, he's . . ." Boss snaps his fingers, trying to conjure the word.

"Authentic?" A whisper.

Boss points his finger like a gun. "Bingo. Look, if another pod opens up, I'll call you."

"You gave him my pod?"

Boss's head snaps up, wary. You must have yelled that. He reaches over to tap a button on his phone and call Security.

"Wait!" you protest.

But the men in uniforms are already there to escort you out.

You can't go home to Teresa. You just can't. So you head to the Hey U.S.A. It's a different crowd than you're used to. An afternoon crowd. Heavy boozers and people without jobs. You laugh because you fit right in.

The guys next to you are doing shots. Tiny glasses of rheumy dark liquor lined up in a row. You haven't done shots since college but when one of the men offers you one, you take it. Choke on the cheap whiskey that burns down your throat. Two more and the edges of your panic start to blur soft and tolerable. You can't remember what time it is when you get up to leave, but the Big Chief is bright in the night sky.

You stumble through the door and run smack into DarAnne. She growls at you, and you try to stutter out an apology but a heavy hand comes down on your shoulder before you get the words out.

"This asshole bothering you?"

You recognize that voice. "White Wolf?" It's him. But he looks different to you. Something you can't quite place. Maybe it's the ribbon shirt he's wearing, or the bone choker around his neck. Is his skin a little tanner than it was last week?

"Do you know this guy?" DarAnne asks, and you think she's talking to you but her head is turned toward White Wolf.

"Never seen him," White Wolf says as he stares you down, and under that confident glare you almost believe him. Almost forget that you've told this man things about you even Theresa doesn't know.

"It's me," you protest, but your voice comes out in a whiskey-slurred squeak that doesn't even sound like you.

"Fucking glonnies," DarAnne mutters as she pushes past you. "Always making a scene."

"I think you better go, buddy," White Wolf says. Not unkindly, if you were in fact strangers, if you weren't actually buddies. But you are, and you clutch at his shirtsleeve, shouting something about friendship and Theresa and then the world melts into a blur until you feel the hard slap of concrete against your shoulder and the taste of blood on your lip where you bit it and a solid kick to your gut until the whiskey comes up the way it went down and then the Big Chief is blinking at you, How, How, How, until the darkness comes to claim you and the lights all flicker out.

You wake up in the gutter. The fucking gutter. With your head aching and your mouth as dry and rotted as month-old roadkill. The sun is up, Arizona fire beating across your skin. Your clothes are filthy, your shoes are missing, and there's a smear of blood down your chin and drying flakes in the creases of your neck. Your hands are chapped raw. And you can't remember why.

But then you do.

And the humiliation sits heavy on your bruised-up shoulder, a dark shame that defies the desert sun. Your job. DarAnne ignoring you like that. White Wolf kicking your ass. And you out all night, drunk in a downtown gutter. It all feels like a terrible dream, like the worst kind. The ones you can't wake up from because it's real life.

Your car isn't where you left it, likely towed with the street sweepers, so you trudge your way home on sock feet. Three miles on asphalt streets until you see your highly mortgaged three-bedroom ranch. And for once the place looks beautiful, like the day you bought it. Tears gather in your eyes as you push open the door.

"Theresa," you call. She's going to be pissed, and you're going to have to talk fast, explain the whole drinking thing (it was one time!) and getting fired (I'll find a new job, I promise), but right now all you want is to wrap her in your arms and let her rose scent fill your nose like good medicine.

"Theresa," you call again, as you limp through the living room. Veer off to look in the bedroom, check behind the closed bathroom door. But what you see in the bathroom makes you pause. Things are missing. Her toothbrush, the pack of birth control, contact lens solution.

"Theresa!?" and this time you are close to panic as you hobble down the hall to the kitchen.

The smell hits you first. The scent of fresh coffee, bright and familiar.

When you see the person sitting calmly at the kitchen table, their back to you, you relax. But it's not Theresa.

He turns slightly, enough so you can catch his profile, and says, "Come on in, Jesse."

"What the fuck are you doing here?"

White Wolf winces, as if your words hurt him. "You better have a seat."

"What did you do to my wife?!"

"I didn't do anything to your wife." He picks up a small folded piece of paper, holds it out. You snatch it from his fingers and move so you can see his face. The note in your hand feels like wildfire, something with the potential to sear you to the bone. You want to rip it wide open, you want to flee before its revelations scar you. You ache to read it now, now, but you won't give him the satisfaction of your desperation.

"So now you remember me," you huff.

"I apologize for that. But you were making a scene and I couldn't have you upsetting DarAnne."

You want to ask how he knows DarAnne, how he was there with her in the first place. But you already know. Boss said the new guy's name was Wolf.

"You're a real son of a bitch, you know that?"

White Wolf looks away from you, that same pained look on his face. Like you're embarrassing yourself again. "Why don't you help yourself to some coffee," he says, gesturing to the coffeepot. Your coffeepot.

"I don't need your permission to get coffee in my own house," you shout.

"Okay," he says, leaning back. You can't help but notice how handsome he looks, his dark hair a little longer, the choker on his neck setting off the arch of his high cheekbones.

You take your time getting coffee—sugar, creamer, which you would never usually take—before you drop into the seat across from him. Only then do you open the note, hands trembling, dread twisting hard in your gut.

"She's gone to her mother's," White Wolf explains as you read the same words on the page. "For her own safety. She wants you out by the time she gets back."

"What did you tell her?"

"Only the truth. That you got yourself fired, that you were on a bender, drunk in some alleyway downtown like a bad stereotype." He leans in. "You've been gone for two days."

You blink. It's true, but it's not true, too.

"Theresa wouldn't . . ." But she would, wouldn't she? She'd said it a million times, given you a million chances.

"She needs a real man, Jesse. Someone who can take care of her."

"And that's you?" You muster all the scorn you can when you say that, but it comes out more a question than a judgment. You remember how you gave him the benefit of the doubt on that whole Cherokee thing, how you thought "pretendian" was cruel.

He clears his throat. Stands.

"It's time for you to go," he says. "I promised Theresa you'd be gone, and I've got to get to work soon." Something about him seems to expand, to take up the space you once occupied. Until you feel small, superfluous.

"Did you ever think," he says, his voice thoughtful, his head tilted to study you like a strange foreign body, "that maybe this is my experience, and you're the tourist here?"

"This is my house," you protest, but you're not sure you believe it now. Your head hurts. The coffee in your hand is already cold. How long have you been sitting here? Your thoughts blur to histories, your words become nothing more than forgotten facts and half-truths. Your heart, a dusty repository for lost loves and desires never realized.

"Not anymore," he says.

Nausea rolls over you. That same stretching sensation you get when you Relocate out of an Experience.

Whiplash, and then . . .

You let go.

A HARVEST OF BEATING HEARTS

Never fall in love with a deer woman. Deer women are wild and without reason. Their lips are soft as evensong, their skin dark as the mysteries of a moonless forest. A deer woman will make you do terrible things for a chance to dip your fingers inside her, to have her taste linger on your tongue. You will weep before it is over, the cries of one who has no relatives. But you will do whatever she asks.

"Tansi, Tansi," my lover whispers my name. "Is it time to harvest the hearts?"

The horror of her question is always fresh, always a shock. I suppose in the daylight hours when she is not here, I am able to tell myself that it never happened. That her words are other than what I know them to be. As long as I don't look at what we keep in the old cooler on the fire escape, as long as I ignore her bloody breath.

The hand she rests against my cheek is still damp and smells faintly of rot. The air clots my nose with a coppery sweetness that has become familiar. Her eyes meet mine, vast and luminous. They say that if you gaze into someone's eyes, you can see their soul, but my lover has no soul. Her eyes are mirrors, showing me only myself, and I turn away from what I see. I reach for her instead, my hands compelled by something primal. If desire were a thing made physical, it would be the curve of my lover's neck, the slope of her shoulders. It would taste like the salt of her skin. It would sound like the susurrus of her breath. So, of course I say what I always say, every time she asks me to kill for her.

"Yes."

"We only need a few more hearts now," she says. "Two? Three? I've lost count. Are you counting?"

"Three." Last week when she asked, it was five. The fifth we harvested on a Monday night in the empty parking lot of a deserted travel stop off I-95, a blond-haired clerk whose steps were heavy with minimum wage and payday loan debt. Four was a gray-eyed mother of two, the backbone of her family. She fought hard, a strong heart, a worthy sacrifice, something to break the best of her people.

"They were monsters," my lover says to me. "And it does no good to have mercy on a monster. They will not have mercy on you." She tucks herself against my ribs and rests her head on my shoulder. The silver moonlight through the open window snags in her hair, the light of distant stars caresses her skin. She tilts her face up for a kiss. I lean in, eager, but she moves away, laughing. She rolls to her feet, drags at my hand. "Let's go!"

I go, stumbling out of bed, barefoot across peeling and cold plastic tiles, ignoring the residue of filth that sticks to my soles. I pull on my jeans, an old stained hoodie. Grab the black leather roll of chef knives from the console by the door. Hesitate at the feel of the leather in my hands, the blades of sharp steel unrevealed. And for a moment, I remember. A life before. Before I met my lover.

"It only has one knife right now," my fiancé Jeffery explains as I open the brightly wrapped box. It's a warm day in early September, the heat of summer still idling over upstate New York. He has obviously taken care in the wrapping of this gift, and my usually deft fingers fumble awkwardly with the green ribbon. When I finally crack open the box, I grin. The chef roll is the one I've always wanted, aged leather, smooth and supple with enough compartments to hold a whole catalogue of knives. Butcher and chop and paring.

"I could only afford one knife right now," he repeats, watching my face for disappointment. "But maybe after school, when you come back home. And we get married . . ." He pauses, waits for my reaction. When I offer him nothing but silence, he goes on. "I know one is not enough, but it's a start, right?"

"One knife is a start," I agree. I don't mention the other thing. "Thank you."

We sit a little longer in this impossible place. A bench on a sprawling leafy campus like something out of a movie about bright college years, a wonderland of green sloping hills on the banks of the Hudson. It is more water, and more things that need water to grow, than I have ever seen in my entire life.

"When will you come home?" he asks.

Home. A tiny reservation town that I outgrew the day I won a local cooking contest, then a statewide competition, and then it was a Food Network cook-off show for teen chefs. The red-haired celebrity chef who hosted it took an interest in my talent. Then an interest in other things. Enough that when I demanded more of his time, he found me a scholarship to a culinary school on the other side of the country, far away from his wife and child.

I unfold the leather roll. Draw the solitary butcher knife from its sheath and run my hands across the silver shine of the blade. I press the tip of the knife into the pad of my thumb until blood rises to the surface. I suck the redness from my skin, eyes closed.

"I thought you weren't doing that anymore," Jeffery says, alarm in his voice and eyes on the bloody thumb in my mouth.

"I'm not."

"I mean, it's okay if you are. I just think maybe you should see someone about it? Especially up here. I bet they have great doctors in a place like this." Jeffery babbles on some more about the superior health care available in the Mid-Hudson Valley, but I've already stopped listening. When he finally tapers off I give him a smile.

"I'm not trying to change you," he insists. "I already told you that."

The smile stays firmly in place. "Let me walk you to your car," I say. "It's a long drive back to New Mexico."

Never fall in love with a deer woman. Deer women are cunning and can see the past and the future all at once. Their eyes are deep and still as well water, their legs as long and slender as the high aspens. A deer woman will make you do terrible things for a chance to stroke the back of her knees, to hear her whisper your name. She will promise you home.

We did not meet in a chance encounter in a moonlit wood, in the way of fairy tales. I did not chase her fleeing shadow through a dappled grove of ancient trees to the banks of an enchanted pool. I was not lured away, as is the way of hunters who have, on a solstice eve, somehow become the prey themselves.

I met my lover in a bar on a weekend trip to Manhattan, an impetuous late train from my upstate culinary school down to the city, a solo escape from a mind-numbing week spent on gastronomy etiquette. Spirit dulled by the proper way to sit at a table, the hand to use for the seafood fork, the ordering of stemware. I am lost in their whiteness, drowning in a sea of their buttery sauces and unfamiliar histories, wishing for something known, something to remind me of home. I overhear a boy in class mention a food truck somewhere on the Lower East Side that serves oven bread and prune pastelitos. It feels like a sign.

New York City is big, noisy, a foreign place. But I am not afraid of it. It beckons, asking me to let go, to become someone else. I wander, looking fruitlessly for that truck, until I hear a deep drum beat, a high wailing through the open door of a corner bar.

She is there, wearing white. A dress that leaves her brown shoulders bare, a skirt that gambols lovingly around her long legs to brush the floor. *Another Native?* I think, smiling. *In New York City? What are the chances?*

She dances the kind of dance that draws stares. The dance that reminds you of the whirl of the starry heavens, of places that exist far away from the white man's concrete canyons. She is graceful and undisciplined all at once, an invitation to question one's life choices.

When she stops, she falls into the high-backed chair next to me at the bar, laughing and flushed. She ignores the others, men and women, who crowd around her offering to buy her a drink. She looks at me.

And I make the mistake of looking back.

We drink St-Germain. Her, neat, in a shot glass, because she says it's like a shot of summer straight to the vein. I take mine with gin, ice, and lemon and agree. We drink, and then we dance, until the night moves on without us and the bartender calls last call. And laughing, dizzy, reckless, we share a nectar-tinged kiss. I should have known then, but in the way of new lust, all I could know was the slip of her hips and the flirt of her long fingers. The flavor of white flowers staining her lips.

Now I understand, in the way of those doomed, that I was being seduced. But like all fools whose desires leave them dashed upon rocks or lost in a faerie's lair, knowledge comes too late for salvation.

I never find that food truck that tasted like home.

The first time she convinces me to kill for her, it is a hot June evening. The sun has already set but the oppressive humidity refuses to allow the day to cool, so we idle, naked, in my bed, eating ice chips and huddling in front of the fan. The first year of school is done but instead of going back to New Mexico and Jeffery, I'm working an internship at a prestigious midtown restaurant. Long hours of back-breaking work for almost nothing. I sleep days and spend my nights in the fury of the kitchen or, on my rare nights off, in her arms. I am in love. I am naïve.

"Why do you only visit me at night?" I ask her. I trace the delicate lines of her back with a finger, brush her hair away from her face. I keep my voice light, teasing. "Maybe we should try to do something during the day."

She rolls over to face me. "Like what?"

"Go to Central Park. Catch a movie."

She groans and flops on her back.

"It's just a thought."

She waves a hand weakly in the air, clearing away my "just a thought." "Tell me about your people, Tansi."

"What do you mean?" We haven't spoken about our families, neither of us. A strange thing for two Natives to do, but it seemed an understood condition of her attention. Until now.

"Your people back home in New Mexico," she repeats. "Your family."

"We don't talk. They wouldn't approve. If they knew about us—"

"My family is gone," she says, her face focused on the ceiling. She pulls a hair from her head, stretches it out above her. "They were murdered. A long time ago. But sometimes, it feels like only yesterday."

"I'm sorry," I stutter out, shocked at her confession.

She drops the strand of hair and rolls to face me, her dark eyes intent. "Tell me. What would you do if people murdered your family?"

"What do you mean?"

"What would you do? Justice? Revenge?"

"Justice, I guess." I'm still reeling, trying to find my way through the sudden thorns of this conversation. "Revenge sounds scary," I add lightly, a poor attempt to laugh off her black mood.

"Whatever you call it, you would make it right, wouldn't you? If it was in your power, you would make it right?"

A trickle of fear now. A voice that knows, deep down, that this is not a question lightly asked. That what I say now, it is an oath.

I should run. I should not answer. But I am frozen in the bright headlights.

"Yes."

Her nod is grim, satisfied. "Where are those knives, Tansi?"

"What?"

"The ones you always carry. Your chef knives."

"Here. Well, over there. By the door."

"Tansi." She says my name like a dark secret. "I want you to do something for me."

I don't say anything, breath stuck in my throat.

"I want you to help me make it right."

My hands up to the elbow are covered in blood. My heart is thumping wildly in my chest, but perhaps not as wildly or desperately as it should be for what I have done. Shouldn't I be vomiting? Crying? Shouldn't I feel more than a desire for her blessing?

She smiles and my spirit soars, giddy. She leans forward to catch the drip of blood in her small hands, brings it to her mouth and drinks. Her eyes are bright, dancing flames of wildfire. Her long hair catches the light.

"Did you know the Aztecs could remove a beating heart in less than two minutes? But that took a team. Two men to hold the body still and prone, at just the right angle. Two men to hold the legs. A fifth to remove it."

"I didn't. Know, I mean."

"But you and I, we only need each other." She laughs and twirls, her long white skirt flaring around her, blood soaking the hem. She licks her fingers clean.

"What do we do now?" I ask. At least my voice has the sense to shake, to sound too high with fear. "Will the police come? Will I go to jail?"

"We leave the body here in the forest," she says. "You'd be surprised what deer will eat."

"And this?" I hold up the heart, still warm and pulsing in my hand. Just another piece of meat, organ, and muscle. Not so different from preparing cœur de boeuf. At least, that's what I tell myself.

"We'll collect them, Tansi. For my family. For . . . justice."

I look at the dead white woman at my feet.

"Are you sure this is justice?"

She puts a finger to my lips, then her lips to mine. "I certainly feel better. Don't you?"

After that I don't see my lover for days. I start to forget the screams, the smell, the horror. I go to the movies alone. I wander through Central Park. At night, I am thrown back into the insanity of the kitchen, taught to master fire and sharp steel and the incessant demands of perfectionists. After two weeks without her, I can almost believe it never happened. When the chef invites us all out for afterwork drinks, I go. But I am lonely in the company of my coworkers, a foreigner unable to follow their words, their jokes all spoken in a language unfamiliar. I make excuses to leave early.

She is waiting for me when I get home. She steps out of her white dress and parts her legs. Runs trembling hands over her breasts. "Please don't leave me, Tansi," she whispers, tears wetting her cheeks. "Please don't leave me."

I miss work the next day. And then the next. A terse voicemail from the restaurant manager, and terser message from the chef de cuisine. I delete them both. Finally, a concerned email from school about my internship status. I don't answer.

We don't leave my bed for a week.

"You're ruined, Tansi," she says, laughing. "Now all you have is me."

Her face dips between my legs and I shudder. She is enough. She is my work. She is my home.

After, she asks, "Is it time to harvest the hearts?"

We're in a parking lot of a Quiklee's. We have stopped to wash the blood from my hands, to clean my knives in the anonymous restrooms. The cooler in the back of the car is heavy and sated.

"Are we done?" I ask.

She nods. Somewhere in the distance, the sound of a police car streaks down the parkway. The summer has become one for the record books. The internet is splashed with the sensational story. Thirteen women missing between the City and upstate New York. All matching a description.

The lampposts flicker, casting shadows across her heart-shaped face. She sighs and runs a hand across my hair, tucks a strand behind my ear. I shudder down to the marrow of my bones. Even now, after all she has made me do for her, I want her.

"Let's go home now," I beg.

"And where is that, Tansi?"

"Wherever. Just . . . somewhere. We don't have to do this anymore, right?"

She leaves her hand but turns her head away from me, eyes toward the dark night, the myriad trails that vivisect the forest beyond the parking lot. The call of the wind through the thick trees that line the parkway.

"Home," she says, her voice breaking with sorrow. "I want my home back too."

—

Our last night together, while we're still in my little Brooklyn walk-up and whatever comes next is still a sunrise and sunset away, she pulls something from her bag. A notebook, its velvet cover the deep green of secrets.

"I've been keeping a list," she says. "Of my family that were murdered."

She thrusts it toward me. The pages are full of tiny, practiced handwriting. Name after name. Wessagusset. Pamunkey. Massapequa. Pound Ridge. Susquehannock. Great Swamp. Occoneechee. I flip the page, and then another. Another. Skull Valley. Sand Creek. Wounded Knee.

The roar in my head is grief, wide and vast enough to drown whole new worlds. I know it is not mine, but hers. The book tumbles from my shaking hand. "I'm so sorry . . ."

"I felt them all when they died," she whispers, a hand to her heart, her eyes lined with tears. "Every one."

Her dark eyes find mine and she whispers the truth.

"Revenge."

I lug the full cooler across the National Mall, past the band playing "The Star-Spangled Banner," the screaming children with their Rocket Pops, the picnics and laughter and shouting masses waiting for sunset and the promised fireworks.

"What if this doesn't work?" I ask, nerves making my voice rattle. "What if it doesn't bring your home back? What if it doesn't quiet the dead?"

I watch her ponder my questions for a moment. The night holds its breath. On its exhale she laughs, as free and enchanting as a rushing mountain stream.

"But, Tansi, what if it does?"

I place the last heart on the grass. Turn to where she lies sprawled in the middle of the circle. Some curious tourists are already starting to come closer, to see what ancient spell I am working with blood and muscle and grief on this most American of holidays. It is only a matter of time now.

I stretch out beside her. Gather her close to me, breathe in her scent for the last time.

"Are you sad?" she asks.

"No," I whisper, and it's true, but not. "Only that I will miss you," I say, picking words so inadequate they rise to the level of a lie. "Do I have to go?"

She draws a finger across my mouth and I taste the salt of my own tears.

I close my eyes and the children are gone, their melting popsicles only memories discarded on the lawn. The fireworks, reduced to suggestions of smoky trails in a blackening sky. The curious tourists, the monuments, the city. All vanished.

Time, rolled back to silence.

"Are they all gone?" I ask.

"Keep your eyes closed and they are gone."

"And your family?"

"They cannot come back, but their children are still here."

"Then we're home?"

When she doesn't answer, I open my eyes.

I am alone on the lawn. The crowd rushes back in, the noise, the children, the tourists, the smoke, the screams of horror, the sound of sirens.

When they ask you, you must tell them why I did it.

How I fell in love with a deer woman, and deer women taste of elderflower. How deer women are worshiped by the night. How deer women dance wild, wearing dresses made of snow.

They will say that I was found lying alone in the grass, encircled by human hearts on the National Mall. How I am a monster, or worse, a radical. Insane.

Yet they are the ones who trample homelands to mud, slick with the blood of my kin. And still they do not see the bend of the grass, the delicate hoofprints left in the turned earth.

Those you tell will shake their heads and scour my history for signs that I was always a murderer. A childhood of acting out, a record of self-harm, a string of men. But they have never danced salsa in a bar, the taste of honey and lemon on their lips, never drank deep from wells of moonlight, never loved like I did.

They will watch the old Food Network show, which will go into reruns. They will interview Jeffery. They will interview the newly divorced celebrity chef.

And they will never notice the small cracks in the foundation of their nation until it is too late. Until the medicine has taken root. And when they finally do notice, they will never suspect that the hearts of their women were their undoing.

Love a deer woman. Deer women are wild and without reason. A deer woman will make you do terrible things for a chance to raise up a nation, to lie down with a dream. You will weep before it is over, the tears of the blessed, the cries of one who has found lost relatives. And if they ever let you out of your cell, tell them that you would do it all over again.

WHEREIN ABIGAIL FIELDS RECALLS HER FIRST DEATH, AND, SUBSEQUENTLY, HER BEST LIFE

NEW MEXICO TERRITORY.
1880s. WINTER.

Abigail Fields was dying. Slowly, terribly, the gunshot wound in her stomach leaking, her lagging heart stretching too long between beats.

The man who had shot her was named Barton Smalls. He was a coward of a white man, and he had abandoned her on the ice-crusted dirt road outside the all-Black settlement of Pueblo Libre to die, no doubt believing that she would expire in the course of time and worry him no more.

Abby hated to admit he might have the right of it.

Breath was getting harder to come by; the space between inhale and exhale as wide as the Rio Grande where it cut through the high desert just below town and the far shore could barely be seen. But Abby kept on breathing anyway, hoping that Mo would come. That anyone would come. But Mo, especially, as she'd like it to be her lovely brown face she saw last in this world.

She imagined there weren't too many folks like her and Mo in heaven. Nothing in the Bible they'd made her read at the old nun house said much about Black girls making it to the right hand of the Lord, at least to hear those old white spinsters at the nunnery tell it. If Abigail was honest with herself, the life she'd led so far was just as likely to land her somewhere a bit hotter, anyway. Good, then. Hell suited her just fine. Just fine, indeed.

A distant howl broke her from her reverie, followed by a mob of high-pitched yips. A shiver of fear rolled through her body, but all she could do was blink up at the gray winter sky above her. Catch the snow-capped tops of the distant mountain range out of the corner of her eye. Feel the rough touch of dirt and the wet of melting snow beneath her back. And try to keep breathing.

Snow fell, soft and silent. Too silent.

Silent meant everyone else in town was dead. Jolene at the schoolhouse and Francis and Lucy who ran the post. Mr. Henderson and Rose and Rose's sisters. Oh, and their little ones, too.

Even Mo? No, not Mo. She'd been out hunting this morning, shooting grouse to fill their table. She was miles away. Should have been, at least. But she was expected back by now, wasn't she? Oh Lord, not Mo. It would be too much.

Another howl, closer now. Coyotes, out there in the distance. Scavengers, tricksters. Likely coming to this little township that was now only a buffet of fresh death. Perhaps it would be the scavengers and not Smalls's gunshot that took her life. Just like what had happened to her great-aunt Mary, only Mary had survived a wolf attack and lived to tell the tale. But then Aunt Mary was a legend, and what was Abby but a sixteen-year-old girl, shot in the belly by a coward of a white man, waiting to die?

Part of her thought maybe she'd drawn Barton Smalls to her. Of all the places in all the settlements west of the Mississippi, she'd never thought to see him again. He had looked right at her when he pulled that trigger, and then looked away, her face unrecognized, unremembered. But she remembered him. There was a penny in her pocket to make sure she always remembered.

"Let me live, Lord," Abby whispered through cracked and bloody lips. "If you let me live, I will murder Barton Smalls. I will forsake love and match him hate for hate. Save me, and I will become an instrument of your vengeance. I swear it!"

It was a bold prayer, and who was Abby to make it? She was not particularly brave. Not a gunslinger. Just a girl and not quite a woman, at that. But she was determined, and she meant it with all her heart, and sometimes, and in some places, that's enough.

It went without saying that hate and vengeance were not a sentiment she'd learned from the nuns at the convent, so their God did not hear her. But there were other things in the desert listening. They did not mind hate, they held no fault with vengeance. They found her offering pleasing and struck the deal.

Abigail knew the moment it happened. She felt the covenant take root in her bones. Her breathing eased, the wound in her side knit closed, her heartbeat became strong and steady.

She thought to cry out, and perhaps she did, with only the scavengers and tricksters and the dead to hear her.

And that, too, was enough.

The sun crawled across the sky and Abby faded in and out of consciousness. After a while, she felt something heavy and warm fall across her body. The smell of wool and smoke filled her nose, and strong arms wrapped around her and lifted her up. They pressed her against warm skin, a wide chest. Her eyelids fluttered open. Deep brown eyes met hers, concern and relief battling in a lopsided grin. Mo's face was blood-spattered. Her own? Or someone else's?

"Now aren't you a blessed sight," Abby murmured.

"Shhh," Mo said, her voice as warm and soft as the blanket she had wrapped her in. "I came as fast as I could. I'm so sorry, Abby. I should have never left you." Mo was breathing hard, fear etched in her face. Her hand hovered over the blood-soaked place on the front of Abby's dress. "Are you hurt?"

"Nothing bad," she lied. "Only grazed."

"I better check the wound . . ."

"No!"

Abby calmed her voice. Mo's hand hadn't even moved. She wouldn't touch her without her say-so. Such manners.

"It's not necessary for you to fuss," Abby said lightly. She knew even if Mo looked, she'd find no trace of the bullet that had rent Abby earlier. The wound was gone, that was a fact.

"I'm shook up, Mo, but I'm fine. Just take me home."

"Of course," Mo said, abashed at her delay.

Abby slipped her arm around Mo's neck to pull close to her. "Is anyone else alive? Jolene? Francis? Rose and her sisters?"

Mo's face was as bleak as the Rocky Mountains behind them. "They're all dead."

"Oh."

"I'm sorry, Abby." Her voice hitched. "It's too lawless out here.

We'll have to move on. To somewhere with a lawman, a real town with a sheriff to protect us."

"No. Lawmen won't fix this. They cause more trouble than they cure and you know that's true. We've got to do this ourselves."

Mo fell silent, as she always did when Abby got it in her head about the evils of white men. But Mo hadn't seen that kind of ugliness firsthand like Abby had, hadn't watched what a mob could do. Of course, there was more to it, this time.

There was Barton Smalls . . . and there was a promise.

She didn't tell Mo of the pact she'd made with the desert. She knew Mo would disapprove of any truck with spirits. The nuns had done more of a brainwash on Mo than she'd cared to admit. Plus, any scheme that put Abby in danger would worry her. That was one of the things Abby liked best about Mo: her worry. And once Mo knew what she had planned for Barton Smalls, Mo would be worried plenty.

"Take it," Great-Aunt Mary had insisted the day Abby left the nun house where her auntie worked. "Take it and use it. This gun don't miss."

"All guns miss," Abby scoffed.

"This one won't," Aunt Mary said, her voice made rough from whiskey and homemade cigars. "It's special. Kept me alive against a pack of wolves."

Abby laughed and adjusted her ladies' hat. It was a fine piece, made all of lace and silk and no other girl in the convent had anything like it. Certainly not her aunt, whom she loved dearly but whom Abby found a bit plain and uncouth. "Ladies don't carry guns."

"Take it, Abigail." She thrust the revolver into her hands. "And when the wolves come for you, you'll know what to do."

Abby had taken it to be polite. After all, they were family. And perhaps she could sell the thing once her and Mo arrived in Pueblo Libre.

She'd put the gun in a box and put the box in her steamer trunk and forgotten about it, mostly. So when the predators did come for her, she hadn't been ready.

"Wake up, Abby," Mo's voice called excitedly from the other room.

The command was followed by a series of booms and bangs and a mild swear as something heavy struck the old pine floor. The dining room chair. Mo had a habit of knocking it over when she was excited.

"What in the world . . . ?" Abby murmured, sitting up in bed. It had been a month since Barton Smalls had razed Pueblo Libre, killing all but two of its residents. In that month, Mo had begged her a dozen times to leave. To move north to Trinidad or all the way up to Denver, where the mines were bustling and there was work to be had in the laundries and saloons. But Abby had refused.

"How do you think they'll treat us there?" Abby had asked. "Two young Black women on their own, and no proper male guardian? And not a dress in sight for you. They'll figure us out lickety-split, and then what?"

"It's safer there . . ."

"Safer for whom?" Abby asked, unrelenting, even though Mo was beginning to droop. "Not us, Mo."

"But if we keep our heads down, don't cause trouble."

"No place is safer than right here," she lied, thinking only of her covenant and the blood she owed the desert. "So we're staying."

"Abby, be reasonable."

"You don't like it, then you're free to go!"

The words were an angry snarl and Abby didn't mean them. Lord, she'd like to die if Mo left her. But she had made promises that couldn't be broken, and the reckoning was coming. She could feel it in the soles of her feet when she walked the open desert, in the cries of birds that circled the small graveyard where they had buried the dead, in the rush of wind through the door that Mo had left open in her haste. And when her palm cupped around her penny.

"Abby!" Mo called again as she burst into the bedroom. She had an envelope in her hand. Not too large, but not small either. Whatever was in there was making Mo dance with excitement like she had bees in her bonnet. She chuckled to herself. Mo in a bonnet? That would be a sight.

"What is it?"

"I got you a present. Well, us. I got us a present." The girl was practically bouncing in place as she presented the packet to Abby. Abby grinned.

"What is it?"

"Open it!"

Abby kept a small knife in her pocket, and she slid it out now to slice open the envelope. Mo's joy was infectious, and Abby couldn't help but grin along . . . until she saw what was inside.

"A ticket to Los Angeles?"

"Two tickets. One for me and one for you."

"Mo—"

"Now, don't say no yet," Mo rushed on. "I know you're not keen on Colorado, but Los Angeles was founded by Black folks just like us. It's a place we could be welcomed. And it's right near the ocean. You told me you always wanted to see the ocean."

"I do," Abby admitted.

"See? And the new train tracks the Santa Fe Railroad built go right there. And it took some doing, but I got us tickets. We leave tomorrow. We can start over. Live how we want to live." She grasped Abby by the arms. "Come with me Abby. Say yes!"

Abby wanted to. So much so that her heart hurt just thinking about saying no. But no is what she had to say.

"Why not!?" Mo cried, throwing her hands up in frustration. "What is so special about staying here? What hold does this place have over you?"

Abby opened her mouth, but she didn't have to answer. The desert answered for her, with a gale of hot wind on a winter's day, the chorus of coyote song, a low rumble of thunder across the mountains.

Mo rubbed her arms, chilled despite the gust of heat, and looked out the window. "Is someone coming?" she whispered.

Abby didn't have to answer that, either.

"A gun, Abby?" Mo cried.

"Not just any gun," Abby countered, lifting the box that held the revolver from her steamer where it had laid since they'd come to Pueblo Libre. "A special gun."

"All guns are the same."

"This was a gift from my great-aunt Mary. She told me it couldn't miss."

"All guns miss."

Abby grinned. "That's what I told her, too."

"Barton Smalls is an outlaw, and a sharpshooter by reputation. Plus, he won't come alone, Abby. To face him and his men down with one gun? It's suicide."

"I'm not afraid of a little death."

Mo threw up her hands. "There is a perfectly good train ticket to somewhere green and beautiful and safe lying on the kitchen table. Pick it up and claim it and come with me!"

Abby opened the chamber of the .38 revolver. "You know they call this gun the Lemon Squeezer," she told Mo. "On account of the way you have to squeeze the grip to pull the trigger."

Mo stared at her. "Are you even listening to me?"

"I already told you—"

"I know. Your great-aunt Mary. She would have stayed and fought. But she ain't here. And, besides, that's a maybe. You don't know. She might have gone to Los Angeles, too."

Abby smiled, sadness warring with resignation.

The other girl deflated like somebody had let the air out of her. "Please come."

"Maybe in the spring. After I've taken care of things here."

"You can't stay here alone. Who's gonna keep you safe?"

Abby patted the box that held the revolver. "Aunt Mary."

The walk back from the train station was long and lonely. Tearful promises had been made. Not the kind a dying girl makes to the desert. The kind two girls in love make to each other. Hopeful, full of dreams.

I have forsaken love, Abby thought to herself, *for a chance at revenge.*

Soon, the desert whispered. And the desert never lied.

Barton Smalls was in her dreams. Not looking as he had been when he'd rode into Pueblo Libre, but as he had been back in Texas, when

Abby still lived with her mama and hadn't been sent to Aunt Mary's and the nuns yet. Young, light-haired, and dark-eyed, a handsome man, at least in her child's eye.

He'd been one of the men who'd come for her daddy. Not screaming and ugly like the others, their voices screeching demands for blood, but he was there just the same, guilty just the same. Smalls had watched them take Daddy away, and when he'd seen her watching him, he'd flipped her a penny. A real copper penny. And laughed as it fell at her feet.

She'd never forgotten his face or that contemptuous penny . . . or the star he'd worn on his chest. And she'd never told Mo about any of it, how Smalls was the reason she knew lawmen couldn't be trusted, that you couldn't find safety in town. That maybe there was no safety but the kind you made yourself, and even that had a way of failing sometimes. But then maybe safety was overrated, and a girl had to embrace danger if she wanted to survive. And maybe survival itself was overrated and a girl had not to fear death, and that's the best she could do sometimes.

Abby awoke with a start. Bolted straight out of bed like the devil was on her heels, and maybe he was.

Barton Smalls was coming.

She fumbled the covers away, dressed hurriedly in trousers and a long coat. The Lemon Squeezer rested in its box, and she claimed it and the single bullet, chambering it before she left the house.

The sun was barely a glow of white on the horizon when she came to the road. She stood resolute in the very place he had left her to die. The earth knew her, recognized her by blood and bone and welcomed her back. To finish what had been started.

Mo was wrong.

Barton Smalls came alone. Riding a white horse and wearing a white church suit, a pale rider on a white horse.

His hair was unkempt and his eyes were wild. There were places on his face where he had scratched the skin clean off and sores ran yellow with pus. His frame was skeleton-thin, and his hands trembled around the reins that threatened to fall from loose fingers.

Abby paused. This was the man that had almost ended her life? That had haunted her nightmares and kept her from her love? This was the thing she had feared since she was a child?

"What's wrong with you?" she asked, her voice carrying across the emptiness between them.

Barton didn't answer, and at first, she thought he didn't hear her. But his brow lifted, and his eyes turned in her direction and the corners of his mouth tilted up.

"Don't I know you?" he asked in a voice slurred from pain and drink and the business of dying.

Abby took a step back, horrified. Had he finally recognized her? The penny was hot in her pocket, next to the Lemon Squeezer.

Barton's head rolled on his neck. "Don't I know this place?"

"You have a sickness," Abby shouted, raising the revolver. "The plague . . ." But even as she said it, she knew that wasn't it. The desert stripped a man of his pretenses. Barton Smalls had always been rotten underneath, only now it showed through.

"They're all dead," Barton said, his gaze falling earthward. "Old Charlie and Dewey and the other boys. All dead."

"Then why'd you come?"

"The desert's been calling my name."

Abby gasped. Could it be her? The covenant she made? Or even . . .

"Do you know who I am?" she asked. "Do you recognize my face?"

He peered at her, leaning precariously over his horse, and she held her breath, waiting. After a moment, he shook his head. "I can't say I do."

In a way it was a relief, she supposed. It meant he hadn't come to Pueblo Libre because of her. This was just another Black settlement to terrorize for him, her friends here just nameless lives stolen.

She still held the gun, but she was unsure now what to do. Now that the moment had come, it didn't tempt like it had before. Smalls was rotten, inside and out, and she need not end his life to prove that.

Her free hand went to the penny in her pocket. She thought about giving it back. Throwing it in his face. Screaming that he might not remember her, but she sure as hell remembered him. And then pulling the trigger on the Lemon Squeezer to make it bark lead until Barton Smalls was dead.

But she also thought of Mo's eyes when she'd boarded that train. The way her entire face had flushed hot when she leaned in to kiss her. Even though it was chaste, a brush of lips against her cheek, it was enough to make Abby warm.

Mo, who had believed in a future. Mo, who even now was somewhere far from the desert. Mo, who would not want this man's death to stain her hands.

Abby lowered the gun.

"I'm too good for you, Barton Smalls. You stay right here and rot away and die. Let the desert keep calling your name until it swallows you whole. I'm done with it."

And she turned her back on Barton Smalls.

The desert pulled at her feet, whispered words of covenant,

dark promises, stolen life that she had bartered for but had not yet earned. Distant howls broke across the Rio Grande in the valley below town.

You owe us, it said. *A life for a life. You promised!*

The rumble started far off and closed in fast. It took Barton by surprise, knocking him from his horse. He lay unmoving on the ground, on the road where he'd once left her. She watched in horror as he seemed to deflate, the life draining out of him. And then his skin bubbled and split and filled again, but not with Barton Smalls. Something else inhabited his body now, and it rose up on coltish legs and reached out overlong arms and blew hot breath across her face. Colorless eyes caught her gaze and a gaping hole of a mouth spoke.

You promised!

"You have your life," she said. "Take Smalls and be done with me."

Still hungry, and you promissssssed!

The creature was greedy, and Abby was not impressed. She raised the Lemon Squeezer, the gun Aunt Mary said never missed. Pointed it at the thing that had been Barton Smalls.

"I changed my mind."

She pulled the trigger.

"Good morning, ma'am," the conductor greeted her as she stepped on the train. He motioned for the younger man next to him to take her steamer, and he dutifully complied. Abby handed him her ticket for inspection. "You heading to Los Angeles?"

Abby nodded.

"You have friends there?"

"Someone special who I hope will be my family someday."

"A sweetheart," he said with a knowing wink. "Well, they'll be mighty happy to see you." He gestured down the aisle, indicating the seat assigned to her. "Get comfortable, and I'll let you know when supper is served."

"How long is the trip?" she asked, taking her seat.

"Not too long. And the scenery is quite something. We'll pass right by the Grand Canyon."

Abby dug into her pocket and flipped the young man who took her steamer a penny. He grabbed it out of the air and bobbed his head, grateful for the tip. Abby pulled down the window shade.

"I don't much care for the desert scenery," she said, "but I'm quite looking forward to the ocean."

THE BOYS FROM BLOOD RIVER

"It's just a song, Lukas," Neveah says, her voice heavy with disdain. "Nobody believes the Blood River Boys will actually appear if you sing it." She leans a plump hip against the old-fashioned jukebox that squats in the corner of Landry's Diner and runs a bright blue fingernail down the playlist, looking for just the right song to get us through after-hours cleanup.

I lean on the broom in my hands and watch her. She's so confident. So easy in her body. Where I'm . . . not. I'm too skinny, too gangly, too tall. Caught somewhere between baby bird and Slender Man, if Slender Man were a pock-faced sixteen-year-old boy whose hair wouldn't lie flat no matter how much gel he slathered on it. If Slender Man weren't even the least bit cool.

"Your brother believes," I offer.

She shakes her head. "Honestly, Brandon is the last person in the world who knows anything about the history of Blood River, much less something like the Boys."

Her eyes dart to me, then quickly away. I know she's avoiding looking directly at me, as if not making eye contact will mean she doesn't have to acknowledge the purpling bruise circling my left eye. As if not seeing my black eye means I don't actually have one.

But not acknowledging something doesn't make it go away. Most of the time it makes it worse.

"You don't believe in the Boys, do you?" Neveah asks me.

Neveah works here at the diner with me, and she's the closest thing I have to a friend, but even she's not my friend. Not really. She's older than me, almost graduated from the community college, whereas I have another full year of high school. If I were going to high school, that is. I'm pretty close to dropping out. Neveah's smart, way smarter than me. But she's wrong about the Boys.

"Brandon sure knew all the details," I challenge nervously. I don't want to make her mad at me. She's pretty much the only person in this town that even talks to me. But she's wrong. I know it. "Their escape, their hideout up by the old mine, the things they did when the townspeople came for them."

"What about the song?" she asks, eyes focused back on the jukebox. "Do you believe that part?"

"No." That was the least plausible part. But even as I say no, I wish I were saying yes. "But—"

"Shhh . . . Here's my jam." She punches the little white button and after a few seconds a song starts. But it's not the one I expected.

The slow moan of a fiddle wails from the jukebox, joined by the heavy thump of a washboard drum, and then a banjo, picked strings as soft as a weeping woman. And a man sings: *As I walked by the river, the moon my companion, I spied a young fellow, an amiable lad . . .*

Neveah frowns. "This isn't the song I picked." She slams a hand against the side of the jukebox, but the song plays on.

He'd the face of an angel but the heart of a demon, and that night he did take the lone life that I had.

"It's the Blood River Boys' song," I say, voice high with excitement. "The one we were just talking about!" I'd never heard it before, but it had to be it. Since when did Landry put that on the jukebox?

A thrill rolls down my spine as the fiddle joins the melody with a minor note, and I'm not sure if it's the music or something else that's making the room feel colder and the night darker, out there beyond the thin windowpanes.

"I didn't pick this!" Neveah complains. She slams her hand against the player again. "It just started on its own." She shoots me a suspicious glare. "If this is some kind of sick joke, Lukas . . ."

He said, 'Wrath is my birthright and woe my first swaddling, blood for my feast as I take what is owed . . . The harvest is coming, and we reap what's been sowed.'

"I didn't do it!" I protest, laughing. "You did. If anyone's playing around, it's you."

"Well, you make it stop!" Her voice rises with a touch of hysteria, and I realize she's serious. I drop the broom, letting it clatter to the floor, and take three quick steps so I'm close enough to reach around the back of the jukebox and hit the emergency Off button.

For a minute I think it's not going to shut off, like we're in some horror movie and the thing has a life of its own, but sure enough, the machine cuts off, just like it's supposed to.

Silences rushes in. The lights behind the counter dip with the electrical surge, the neon signs in the windows blink off and then power back on with a high-pitched whine. And something out in the night howls.

My skin prickles as a solid rush of fear rolls up my back. Neveah and I exchange a look.

"We are never letting Brandon tell us scary stories again," she says, firmly rubbing her hands up her arms.

"Sure thing," I say absently, eyes drawn out into the night, searching. But for what, and why exactly, I'm not sure. It's just a feeling . . .

Neveah shudders like it's cold. "I just told you that if you sing the song those freaks are supposed to appear, and then you play it? Don't you think that's a little too much?"

"I told you I didn't do it."

"Well, somebody did!"

A shadow passes by the window. Something's out there, moving through the parking lot. Probably a raccoon or a skunk. But bigger.

"Probably Brandon," Neveah mutters.

"In the parking lot?"

"What? No. It was probably Brandon who set up the song." She peers out the big front windows. "What do you mean 'the parking lot'?"

"Nothing. Just thought I saw animals in the trash." Maybe it was Brandon. Scaring the shit out of us would probably be his idea of fun. But still. How would he have set it up beforehand? And Landry would never go for that sort of thing. She's pretty uptight about the jukebox.

"I want to go home," Neveah says, thrusting her hands in her hoodie pockets. "This is all too much."

I sigh. I want to go home too. The night feels sour now, as if the joke's on us and we're not in on it.

She pulls her phone out of her pocket, swipes it on, and types furiously. "Where is Brandon? I knew he should have waited for my shift to end."

"I can give you a ride." Even as I say it, I'm wincing. Maybe it's too much, too presumptuous. Like I said, we're not really friends.

She glances up, and I can see the calculations run across her face: surprise, suspicion, hesitation, and then finally all that loses to her desire to get out of here as soon as possible.

"Okay, sure. Why not."

I grin, strangely relieved. Maybe being rejected for offering her a ride home would have hurt more than I want to admit. It's not that I like Neveah that way. I don't like any girls that way. She knows that. But I'm the town loser. Nobody wants to spend too much time with a loser. It might rub off.

She bends and picks up the broom where I dropped it, hands it back to me. I gesture toward the rag and spray bottle on the counter. "It'll be faster if you help."

She exhales disapprovingly, but slouches over to the counter, grabs the cleaning supplies, and gets to work. I start sweeping, and we clean in silence, neither of us much wanting to try the jukebox again. But I can't get that song out of my head, and before I know it, we're both humming it.

We realize it at the same time and stop. Neither of us look up, an unspoken agreement to pretend like that didn't just happen, but the horror still lingers on my skin, in the faster-than-normal beat of my heart.

Around midnight, we call it good enough. Neveah helps me put the supplies away, and I let her out the door first, locking up behind her. I pause in the parking lot, eyes scanning for the shadow of movement I saw earlier, but there's nothing there. I tell myself it was probably just a raccoon, like I thought.

—

My old car putters through the empty streets of Blood River. I wouldn't even own a car if I had a choice, but I need a car to get my mom to her weekly doctor's appointments at the hospital in the next town over. That's also why I got the job at Landry's. My paycheck, what little there is of it, goes to paying off this piece of junk and anything left over goes to Mom's medical bills.

Blood River isn't very big. About four square miles of gridded streets. We're two dozen miles from the main highway. It's one of those towns that was important back when the railroad ran through here and the grain silos were full, but now with the big interstates and airplanes and nobody growing grain much anymore, people don't come here. Blood River is what some folks would call a dying town. I mean, there's the diner, and the high school football games are pretty popular on Friday nights, and there are a few places trying to draw in tourists for white-water rafting or fly fishing in the nearby river, but the only thing we're really famous for, what gave the place its name, is a massacre.

Not so popular with tourists.

We pass the old graveyard and drive past overgrown yards and single-story bungalows with paint peeling from the planked sides. I take the corner Neveah tells me to and we roll up to a trailer on blocks and a smattering of dead cars parked haphazardly on the gravel out front.

"This is me," she says.

I pull over. We haven't said much the whole ride.

She opens the passenger-side door. The little light in the ceiling goes on, and I can see her face. Her skin is a peachy white, pretty much the opposite of my brown skin, and her hair is a bottle yellow, showing darker at the roots. Her nails are long and bright blue, little rhinestones embedded on the tips. She pauses, one blue-jeaned leg sticking out, the rest of her body still in the car. She looks over at me, bottom lip caught between her teeth, hazel eyes too big.

"What is it?" I ask, wary.

"Thanks for the ride," she says. "I know people give you a lot of shit for being—"

"Native?"

"Gay."

We both flush hot and embarrassed. The silence stretches like another lonely block of this trash-heap town.

"I'm sorry about your eye," she says in a rush.

My heart speeds up a little, but I frown like I'm not following. "How do you mean?"

"How Jason Winters beat the crap out of you, how he and the Toad Twins always beat the crap out of you. How that's the reason you dropped out of school. Well, that and your mom being sick."

I stare at her blankly, willing her to shut the hell up.

"I figure that's why you love the Blood River Boys story so much. It's like a fantasy, right? The idea of those Boys coming to rescue you from your shitty life in this shitty town."

My face heats up, the flush creeping down my neck. "My being interested in the Blood River Boys has nothing to do with any of that," I lie flatly. "I just like a good story."

"You sure?"

"Positive."

"Because if it were me . . ."

And I know she is not going to take the hint. "Good night, Neveah," I say, reaching over and pushing her door open a little wider.

She frowns.

"Good night!" I repeat.

She leans back into the car and reaches for my arm. I shrink back. It's an automatic response, not personal, but it leaves her hand hovering in the air. The overhead light catches in the tiny rhinestone on her nail. She pulls her arm back and says, "I am trying to be nice to you. Trying to be sympathetic."

"Keep it," I say harshly, and even as the words leave my mouth, I regret them. But I don't know what her kind of "sympathetic" means. It smells like white girl pity to me, and I don't want Neveah's pity. I throw a meaningful glance at her trailer, the beaters in her driveway. *You're not better than me,* I say, without saying a thing. *Just look around.*

Her face twists up, and my stomach slips to my feet like a dead weight. I'm being a jerk and I know it, but I won't walk it back.

She nods once and slides out of the car. Closes the door and the overhead light goes off, casting me back into the darkness.

Shame blankets me and I groan, rubbing a hand over my face. Why did I do that? No wonder I don't have any friends. No wonder Jason Winters likes to kick my face in. I'm kind of an asshole.

I wait for her to walk to her door, and once she's inside, I pull out, gravel rolling under my wheels. I'm halfway down the road, trying desperately to not think about what Neveah said, when I realize I'm humming that song again. The Blood River Boys ballad.

Later, after it is all over, I'll wonder if things would have turned out different if I'd said something. Apologized for being a dick, admitted what I wanted and why the Boys fascinated me, how I felt about my mom and everything. Maybe Neveah could have said something, conjured some words or a warm touch that would have changed things. But I didn't, and she didn't, and things went the way they did in our dying town that was named after a massacre.

—

The next morning I catch myself humming the Blood River Boys song in the shower. And later, as I'm boiling eggs for breakfast. And again when I'm prepping Mom's medications for the day, laying them out in their little individual bowls so she doesn't have to guess the dosage.

And I know I've got to face a hard fact. Neveah may not believe in the Blood River Boys, but I do. I believe in them with my whole heart. A heart that feels like it's slowly crumbling to dust in my chest, a heart so damaged that I sometimes feel like it's a wonder that it pumps at all.

Back last year my heart was normal enough. But then my cousin Wallace died of a drug overdose, and my friend Rocky moved away, back to his dad's place in the city, and then just as the school year started, Mom got sick. At first no one believed Mom's illness was serious, least of all me, but by October she was in and out of the hospital and the doctors were giving her less and less time and then Mom sat me down one night after she had been especially bad, wheezing and coughing through dinner, and told me the truth. She wasn't getting better. In fact, she was getting worse. "This will be our last Christmas together," she said, point blank, just like that. "You'll be eighteen soon enough. Better get used to being on your own."

But the thing is, I don't want to be on my own. Some kids would, I know. They'd see it as independence. Freedom. And it's not like I don't want that, one day, maybe? Just not this year. I mean, I already lost Wallace and Rocky and now it's going to be Mom. And I think that if I'm not careful, I'm going to lose myself next.

—

"Hey, Landry," I ask, as I lay bacon on the flat grill. "When'd you put that Blood River Boys song on the juke?"

Landry's doing the books in her office, but she's got the door open so she can keep an eye on things, namely me. The cook called in sick, so I'm stuck covering the dinner shift in the kitchen. The diner is so small that I do a bit of everything. Janitor, cook, server. I don't mind. It means more money in my pocket come payday and more meds for my mom, and most people's tastes are simple around here. As long as I can break eggs and dress a burger, I'm good.

"What song?" Landry says, decades of cigarette smoke turning her voice to a grumble. "I ain't changed a song on that box since before Ronald Reagan was president."

"No?" I shrug and grab the next waiting ticket. "Maybe I just never saw it. So that means something's wrong with the juke. Neveah was trying to play her song last night and the wires got crossed. Played the wrong song."

Landry gives a noncommittal grunt. I busy myself with the order and once it's done, slide the plate through the little window for the server to pick up. I ring the little bell, and Fiona appears, all smiles. She takes the plate and disappears.

I turn to retrieve the next order and Landry's right there, inches from my face. I yelp in surprise, jumping back a half mile. "Jesus, Landry, don't sneak up on me like that!"

She peers in close. I can see the wrinkles on her face, the rheum that covers her left eye. "That song's only appeared once on that jukebox, and that was before the Finley boy went missing. They say he called it up, and so it came." She narrowed her eyes. "You got a hankering to listen to that song?" she asks, voice hard. "Bad things happen to boys who sing that song."

"No," I say automatically. "I was just telling you what happened. I-I don't want to . . ." I brush my hands together, nervous. "I didn't sing that song."

She peers at me some more. "Okay." And then she shuffles back to her office.

"Why do you have it on the juke if you don't want anyone singing it," I mutter, and if she hears me, she ignores me.

I'm closing again, and this time Brandon's on time to pick up Neveah.

"She's in the bathroom," I say, as I unlock the door to let him in.

He answers with a grunt that could mean anything. He was okay the other night when he was talking about the Boys, but now he barely acknowledges me. Like I said, nobody wants to spend too much time with a loser. But what Landry said is on my mind, so I ask.

"You ever hear of somebody Finley?" I ask, trying to keep my voice neutral.

He's got a wad of tobacco in his mouth and he eyes me, jaw working like a cow chewing cud. "Dru Finley?"

I shrug. "Maybe."

"Everybody knows about Dru Finley. He used to live here, back in the eighties. Big baseball star. Everyone thought he was going to make it to the major leagues. Then, supposedly he snaps one night and kills his whole family, but they never find him or a body. Just his family, exsanguinated. Do you know what that means?"

I shake my head.

"Bloodless," he whispers. "Someone drained all their blood."

"How'd that happen?" I say, my voice breathy.

"Who knows? But the bigger question is what happened to Dru? Maybe he ran when the killers came and never looked back. Maybe he got kidnapped. Nobody knows." He widens his eyes theatrically. "Why do you want to know?"

"No reason. Someone mentioned him today."

"Yeah, well, whatever happened, at least he got out of this shit town, right?" He chuckles at his own bad joke.

Neveah hustles out of the bathroom. "Ready?" she asks Brandon without even looking my way. I guess she hasn't forgiven me for being rude last night. Brandon kind of gives me a nod and then he's following his sister out the door.

Once their car is gone, I lock the door again.

The jukebox glows in the corner.

I walk over and stare at the song selections. My heart is thumping, loud in my ears like a warning sign, but I've been thinking about it all day. I have to know.

My guess is that it doesn't matter what button I push, that they'll all do the same thing. So I close my eyes and reach out a hand. Press a random button and wait.

Fiddle, drums, banjo. And then that voice. *As I walked by the river, the moon my companion, I spied a young fellow, an amiable lad . . .*

And this time, I listen. The whole way through. And when it's done, I play it again, and this time I mouth the words, remember the phrases, the rhyme and rhythm of it. And on the third time, I sing.

I let the words come bubbling from my throat, trickling across my tongue and through my lips, and once I've started, they feel like a flood, like the Blood River itself, a force unstoppable and powerful and ancient. And I put everything into it. All the stuff

I've been feeling about being alone, the injustice of Jason and his friends bullying me, my mom dying, every scared part of me. My crumbling, dusty heart. And I let it all go.

When it's over I feel wrung out. I hobble over and collapse in the nearest booth, panting. Wishing for a cold glass of water, but I'm too tired to walk over and get one.

And I wait.

And . . . nothing.

I wait thirty minutes, and then thirty minutes more, and there's no movement in the parking lot, no dimming lights, no chill. Just me and some scary stories and my wretchedness. I press my cheek against the cool Formica and let the tears leak from my eyes. After a while, I sit up and use my cleaning rag to wipe the tears away.

I get up, my bones feeling a thousand years old. Make it to the car. Drive the empty streets home. Check in on my mom.

I collapse into bed, no different than I was when I started this awful day.

He comes the next day.

I'm back at Landry's Diner. It's late, a half hour until closing, when I notice him. He's in the booth farthest from the door, the four-seater by the jukebox where I'd wept like a little kid the night before. He's wearing a black cowboy hat, which is what I spot first, and a dark denim jacket. He's got boots on, not unusual around these parts, and they're propped up on the opposite seat. They're black, too, and the leather catches the light and makes them gleam.

The brim of his hat is pulled down to cover his face, so all I catch is a sliver of pale skin, and a slice of easy grin as I approach him.

"Kitchen closes in thirty," I say when I'm standing in front of him. I'm on server duty because it's Neveah's night off. I hold my ordering pad up, pen poised.

"Nothing I want is on the menu," he says, his voice an easy drawl. He tips his hat up, shows his face, and I suck in a startled breath. If you asked me to describe him, I couldn't do it. But the curve of his lips, the narrow slide of his nose, the sharp cut of his cheeks. It was a kind of perfection, that much I know.

"Are you on TV?" I blurt. Because no one that looks like this boy has ever come to Blood River before.

He laughs, and even that's beautiful, like the rush of a cold wind on the first day of autumn or the roll of thunder on a hot summer night.

"Naw," he says. "I'm not on TV."

I look over my shoulder, for what, I don't know. A witness, a hidden camera. Jason and the twins playing a trick on me.

"You called to me, Lukas," he drawls. "Don't you remember? You called me with my song and that dusty heart of yours." He throws his arm out expansively. "You called all of us."

I look behind me, again, and sure enough, walking down the aisle are three more boys, all a little older than me. They're all wearing cowboy gear, hats and boots and broken-in denim, except for one kid who's got his baseball cap on backward and is wearing oversized jeans.

"Allow me to introduce my brothers," he says. "This is Jasper, and next to him is Willis. And that there is Dru. And I," he says, with a tip of his hat, "am Silas."

"Are you the . . . ?" But I can't bring myself to ask. I'm afraid if I say it aloud, they'll laugh at me. Or disappear.

"What's good in this joint?" Jasper asks, rattling a menu. He's got a deep voice and some kind of accent I can't quite place. His skin is the same shade as mine, and he's got a head of dark hair under his hat.

"Menu's about the same everywhere we go," Willis says, laughing. His skin's a shade darker than Jasper's and tight black curls peek out from under his hat. His voice is high, nervous, and his black eyes flicker around the room.

"That it is, brother," Silas says with a grin. He slaps a hand on the table. "Let's go somewhere else." He tilts his head. "Won't you come with us, Lukas? Come share a meal."

"Me?" I ask.

The boys laugh, well, Jasper and Willis do. The third boy, a redhead, says nothing. He seems agitated, knee shaking under the table. And Silas, of course, who looks at me solemn as a church song and nods real slow.

"I-I've got to lock up," I stutter.

"Then do that," he says. "We'll wait to eat with you."

This makes Willis laugh, and the redhead shake his head, but I don't get the joke.

Then they're all moving toward the entrance, languid and graceful as cats. I watch them go, convinced I'm hallucinating and will never see them again once they're out the door. The tiny bell over the entrance rings as they slide out, one by one. Silas is last and he tips his hat to me as he crosses the threshold.

My heart is hammering in my chest and I'm not sure what to do but I know I've got to go with them.

"Cook," I yell, rushing around the corner of the counter and pulling my apron off. "My ride's here," I shout, hoping he won't remember I drive myself. "I gotta go."

"What about cleanup?" he asks, sounding outraged.

"Not tonight," I say, grinning. "I'll owe you one."

"You owe me about five," he mutters, but I know he'll do it. Despite his protests, I never ask him for favors.

"Thanks!"

I take a minute to rush to the bathroom, check my face in the mirror, wish desperately for another face, less brown, less skinny, less acne-prone, but then I remember what Silas said, that he came because my heart asked him to. I turn on the faucet, douse my face, and run a wet hand through my hair, trying to make it behave, and then I'm out the door . . .

. . . and run smack into Jason Winters.

"Whoa," he says with his fake laugh, grabbing me by the shoulders to keep me from running right into him. "What's the rush, Lukas?"

I freeze. I can feel his hands on my shoulders, too warm, the pressure of his fingers. I look around the parking lot, frantic. Where's Silas and the others? Where did they go?

"Did you see . . ." I start to ask, then remember who I'm talking to and snap my mouth shut.

Jason looks over his shoulder, and now I see that he's not alone. The Toad Twins are getting out of the back seat of his blue sports car, laughing and heading in our direction. Something catches in my throat. No, no, no. Not now.

"Look," I say, the memory of Silas waiting somewhere out there for me making me crazy bold. "You can pound on my face another time. Right now, I've got to go."

Jason points over my shoulder, back at the diner. "Says Landry's is open another twenty minutes. Me and my boys just want to grab a quick bite. Surely you can help us with that. I mean, isn't that your job?"

The twins have joined us, Tyler and Trey, and they laugh, that same automatic guffaw they always laugh for Jason. Like having a job is a joke.

"Cook's still there. He can help you."

His hands on my shoulders tighten. "I want you to help me."

The way he says it stops me in my tracks even more than the heavy dig of his fingers into my flesh. His eyes meet mine, clear blue like the summer sky, and he smiles.

"I . . ."

"Oh my God," one of the twins says, Tyler or Trey, "he's gonna try to kiss you."

I'm not. Of course I'm not, but my face still burns like it's on fire. I open my mouth to protest but I don't get the chance.

The punch to my stomach is so swift I don't realize he's hit me until I'm bent over double, gasping for air. The second one comes seconds after, a fist to the side of my face just below where my eye's still healing that leaves my ears ringing. I hit the gravel with a thud, the tiny gray pebbles digging into my cheek.

More laughter and I brace myself for the kick that's coming.

"Is there a problem here?"

I'm so wrapped up in my humiliation that it takes me a moment to recognize the voice. I roll my head to the side and look up. Silas is there, black boots and jacket and hat and that easy smile.

Jason sneers. "Mind your own business, cowboy," he says.

"This here is my business. Lukas is my friend."

The three boys laugh. "Lukas Loser? Well, I know you're lying because he doesn't have any friends."

Now the kick comes, right to my gut. It's not as bad as it could have been, as it's been before, but it's enough to make me suck in a breath.

"I thought I asked you to stop," Silas drawls again.

"Or else what?" Jason puffs himself up, broad football player's shoulders almost twice as wide as Silas's slim build.

"Or else I'm going to kill you."

I blink, thinking I must have heard wrong. But there's Silas, cool as the evening air and looking unconcerned, like he's not threatening, just stating facts.

Jason and the Toad Twins gape, first in shock, I think, but then like they're gonna laugh. The other Blood River Boys come melting out of the night. Jasper, quiet and smiling, hands stuffed in his pockets. Willis, his eyes bright, and he chants "Kill you dead, kill you dead" in a breathy, high giggle. Dru dragging farthest behind, his cap turned around to face forward, hiding most of his face in the shadows.

Jason's not a fool. Well, not that kind of fool, at least. He does the math, figures it's four, five if you count me but I'm sure he doesn't, against him and the twins. He raises his hands.

"Sure. Fine. We don't want any trouble. Just came to get something to eat."

"Eat somewhere else from now on," Jasper says in his low, rumbly voice.

"This diner's closed . . . to you," Silas echoes. "Permanently."

Jason glances down at me and I must be smiling because his face goes all dark and furious. "Later, Loser," he mutters. "When your rodeo clown friends aren't around." And then he and the twins are making a hasty retreat.

I laugh, I don't even care that it makes his retreating shoulders tense up and I'm definitely setting myself up for a worse beating when Silas isn't around to save me. It's worth it to see Jason get the smallest taste of the humiliation he doles out to me on the regular.

A hand comes down to help me up and I take it. Silas's palm is cold, dry and icy enough to burn. His skin has a slick glass feel, his flesh stiff. He pulls me to my feet like I weigh even less than I do.

"You all right?" he says, dusting me off. His hands on my body make me nervous, but he acts like he doesn't notice. He looks concerned, like he really cares what happens to me.

"Thanks," I say. "You saved me." And he did, and in more ways than one.

He presses a cold palm to my cheek and for the first time our eyes meet. His are a swirl of color, impossible eyes, eyes like deep pools, a child's kaleidoscope. I blink, sure the blow to my head must be doing something weird to me, and when I look again, his eyes are just their normal brown. Dark, catching the light from the overhead lamp, but totally normal.

"Anything for a brother," he says.

"Shoulda killed them," Willis says.

"Not now," Silas murmurs over his shoulder.

"He's right," Jasper rumbles. "Now we'll have to hunt."

I frown. "What does he mean?"

"Nothing." Silas smiles at me and I feel a flutter in my chest, like my heart wants to answer him with a matching smile. "We've got to go. See you again soon, Lukas. You get home. Take care of that mother of yours. She needs you."

"How do you know about my mother?"

"You told me."

"I didn't . . ."

"See you again soon."

And then they're backing into the night, disappearing into the darkness like they never were. My face throbs where I took the punch and I've got a dull ache in my stomach, but I've never been happier in my life. Pretty sure I could float home. But instead, grinning like an idiot, I climb into my car and head home, singing that song the whole way.

When I pull into the drive, there's someone on the porch. My pulse ticks up, thinking it might be Silas, even though I just left him at the diner, but it's a woman. Middle-aged and looking tired, her cardigan pulled tight around her shoulders against the chill. She seems familiar but I can't quite place why.

"Are you Lukas?" she asks, as soon as I'm within shouting range.

"Yeah. Who are you? And what are you doing at my house at midnight?"

"Delia Day, and I'm sorry about the time," she says. "I'm the patient advocate and social worker at the Bennet City hospital."

That's how I know her. And there's only one reason she would be here at this time of night. "My mom?" I ask, my throat tightening. "Is my mom okay?"

"I'm afraid not, Lukas. You better come inside." Her voice is kind. Too kind. It's the voice professionals use when they're about to give you bad news.

I freeze, not wanting to get any closer.

"Is she at the hospital?" I ask. I'm shaking. When did I start shaking? "Can I go see her?"

Delia rubs at her arms. "Why don't you come inside? We can talk about it in there."

And I know. Right then I know exactly what she's going to say. And I don't want to hear it because hearing it makes it true.

I stumble back to my car. Delia Day is calling my name. I make it down the drive, back onto the street. I don't know where I'm going, what I'm running from, what I'm running to. All I know is that I'm running.

The funeral is short. Mom was adopted and didn't have any brothers or sisters. After she grew up, they lost touch, and my dad was never a presence in our lives, so it really was just her and me.

And now it's just me.

Nobody comes to the funeral except Delia and the county assessor to hand me an envelope I don't want to open, and a few folks from the church that I don't even know but they seem all right. Landry sends her condolences, but she's at the diner working.

Once everyone's gone and it's just me and the fresh grave and the twilight of nightfall, he shows up. He's wearing the same boots, the same denim, the same hat, which he holds in his slender hands. The breeze ruffles his black hair, almost playfully. It just turns mine into a windblown mess.

"Where's the rest of them?" I ask before he's even close.

He stops next to me, eyes on my mother's grave. "Thought maybe it would be best if it's just you and me."

I look over. Stare at the slope of his nose, the fullness of his mouth. My breath hitches, and he smiles.

"The Boys can be a little much," he admits. "Sorry if they scared you."

"They saved me," I say in a rush. "You saved me."

"Jason Winters won't bother you anymore." He says it with such conviction that I almost believe him. But Jason's been bullying me since fourth grade. He's not going to stop just because a couple of cowboys told him to.

"He'll just wait until you're gone," I say quietly, feeling like I'm disappointing him by saying it.

He looks at me, eyes crinkling. "You really are something, Lukas." His voice is wistful, maybe amused, but I don't think he means it as an insult.

We stand there in silence until I say, "I'm alone now."

"You don't have to be."

It's what I wanted him to say but didn't dare hope. I want to shout at him to take me away, get me out of this town, away from the diner and bullies and my empty house. But instead I ask, "What do I have to do?"

"Share a meal."

"What does that mean?"

He looks down, beats his hat against his thigh. "What do you think it means, Lukas?"

I close my eyes. "How? How do I . . . ?"

He touches my shoulder briefly. "We'll take care of that. Just be at the diner tonight at closing. You come if you want to join us. If you don't, no harm and we'll be on our way."

"You'll leave?" I ask, startled, my mouth suddenly dry. "Just like that?"

"Only if you want. You called us, remember? And we only stay where we're wanted."

Relief floods through me, traitorous and unasked for. I can't imagine Silas gone now. What I'd do. Where I'd go. Something about him makes me feel safe, feel wanted. Feel not so alone.

The wind moves through the gravestones, tossing the leaves around. He slips his hat back on.

"The diner," he repeats. "Closing."

And then he's gone.

I pull into Landry's parking lot a quarter to midnight. The lights are low, and the place looks locked up, only there are people moving around inside, so I know somebody's in there. I spot a figure lurking by the door and think it must be Silas, but as I get closer, I can see it's Dru. He's got a baseball bat and he's swinging it idly as he waits. I remember Brandon saying something about the Finley guy being a big baseball player and things click together.

Dru looks at me, long and hard, pale skin cold in the lamplight and dark red hair slicked back. Last time I saw him he was wearing a baseball cap, but tonight he's bareheaded. I shift uncomfortably under his scrutiny.

"Why?" he asks, suddenly, and it's the first time I've heard him speak.

I shrug, pretty sure what he's asking. "Same as everyone, I guess."

"We've all got different reasons. Jasper did it for revenge, me because we didn't make state and I thought I wanted to die." He chuckles under his breath, like he can't believe he was ever so foolish. "Willis went crazy after they killed his wife, and Silas . . ."

"Why did you have to murder your family, though?" I ask quickly, cutting him off. I'm not sure I want to know why Silas did it. What if it's for terrible reasons? Reasons worse than wanting a family, not wanting to be alone.

He blinks. "You think I killed my family? For this?" he asks, incredulous. He laughs a shallow, wheezy laugh. "'Five blood bags, one for each and two for me,' Silas told me."

A shiver runs across my neck. "Silas wouldn't say that."

"What do you know about Silas?" he scoffs. "He's taking it easy on you, don't know why, what makes you so special." He swallows noisily, eyes lost in memory. "He didn't go so easy on me."

I frown. "What do you mean?"

Before he can answer, Silas comes to the door.

"You made it," he said, his smile expansive like I'm on time to his party. "Come on in." He ushers me through the entrance, leaving Dru to follow. I hear Dru turn the lock behind me. I look back, alarmed.

"So we aren't disturbed," Silas says, arm sliding around my shoulders as he leads me in. "I think you know everyone," he says, gesturing around the diner. Dru with his bat and Willis and Jasper on stools and leaning against the counter.

"Listen," I tell him, voice steady with the words I practiced in the car on the drive over. "I know what this is about. What you are." Thinking of what Dru said minutes ago, I add, "You don't have to be easy on me."

Silas pauses, leans his head to the side like he's listening.

I go on in a rush. "I figured it out. What you said about Jason not bothering me anymore, and before saying you'd kill him if he laid a finger on me again. And I know the stories, about the massacre. And Dru's family." My eyes cut briefly to his. His face is stony, giving nothing away, and for a minute I think maybe I've misunderstood, that what I'm saying likely sounds certifiable, but I barrel on anyway. "And I want you to know I'm okay with that. I'm okay with . . . sharing a meal."

Silas waits until he's sure I'm done talking and then smiles. "I knew you'd come around, Lukas. Nothing wrong with going easy on a man who's had his fair share of troubles. Some people just need to be eased into feeding."

Feeding. I shiver, despite myself. The way he says it makes it somehow more real. But I tell myself that Jason deserves it. He's been cruel to me my whole life, would probably kill me if he had the chance, so maybe I'm just beating him to the punch. And if that means I get to stay with Silas, with the Boys . . .

Willis and Jasper stand up to reveal a body laid out on the counter.

I expect to see broad football shoulders. Stupid chestnut hair. Terrified blue eyes.

But instead I see dark roots, the glint of a rhinestone, hazel eyes too wide.

"Neveah?"

I gasp, fall back a step as she whimpers, eyes pleading with me. Willis runs a hand through her hair like he's petting a dog.

"Shhhh," Silas says, holding me in place, his grip like a vice. "I thought you said you were ready."

"Don't hurt her," I say, turning to him. I grasp at his shirt, begging. "I-I thought you meant Jason. Or the Toad Twins. Not—"

My breath catches in my throat.

Not the only person in town who actually tries to be nice to me, not Neveah with her community college and her trailer and her blue nails. Who let me drive her home. Who tried to help.

"We're not going to hurt her, Lukas." His voice is quiet. Firm. And for a minute, I have hope. "You are."

My stomach plummets. I shake my head no, horrified.

"If you want to join us, you have to share a meal."

"I know! I'm here, aren't I? At the diner."

"That's not the kind of meal we eat, brother," Jasper says. I look over and he's picking at his teeth, his fangs, with a long fingernail.

"Don't you get it?" Dru cuts in harshly. "You either drink her blood and become one of us, or you get to be a blood donor, too.

She's a goner for sure, and you're one bad decision away from becoming one. There's no walking out of this."

"Dru speaks the truth," Jasper says, voice deep like the drum in that song. That song that started all this, when all I wanted was someone to rescue me so I wouldn't have to be alone.

I shake my head. "No, I can't. She's my friend. Anyone else."

"You'd rather a stranger die for you?" Silas asks. "Better for it to be a friend. Cut your last ties. Then you're really one of us."

"I don't . . . I don't want this." But it's a lie. I want it. I want it so bad it's making me shake. But Neveah's eyes are on me and she's crying, tears catching on her nose, pooling on the counter.

"You asked us to come," Silas reminds me, hand warm on my back, breath soft in my ear. I feel his lips against my neck, just the slightest touch, but it sends heat through my body that almost brings me to my knees.

"He's sweet on you, Silas," Willis says with a knowing chuckle.

"What do you say, Lukas?" Silas asks. "We could feast, and then you and I could go somewhere private." His hand tightens at my waist. "You won't ever have to be alone again."

It's everything I want. Because I can't go back to that house, to the well-meaning church casseroles and the empty rooms and the organized pill bottles and everything that the county assessor will be through next week to claim.

"I don't want to be alone," I whisper.

"You won't be," Silas says.

And then the jukebox kicks on and the fiddle is playing and that man is singing: *He'd the face of an angel but the heart of a demon . . .*

"Take what's yours, Lukas," he says, "and become one of us."

I take a step forward.

"No!" Suddenly, Dru's there between us. He swings his baseball bat right at Silas, almost too fast for my eyes to follow. The bat connects with the side of Silas's head, shattering into shards. Silas goes down, dazed.

"Run!" he shouts, and I take a hesitant two steps back to the door, my brain trying to make sense of what's going on.

Jasper launches himself at Dru, but the redhead is ready, and he thrusts a shard of baseball bat forward, right into Jasper's chest. He crumbles to ash without making a sound.

"Run, you fool!" Dru shouts again, as Willis jumps onto his back and sinks vicious fangs into his neck. He screams as the blood runs, a river as red as his hair flooding across his throat.

Neveah's on her feet. Whatever was keeping her pinned to the counter, fear or some kind of spell, seems to have broken when Jasper disintegrated. She grabs my hand and pulls me to the door. I stumble after her, eyes still on Willis as he rips Dru's throat out. Dru collapses, eyes clouding over to nothing, head flopping like a broken doll.

I scream. Willis turns toward me, his face no longer that of a beautiful mad boy, but of a monster. He takes a step toward us as Neveah unlocks the door and we stumble across the threshold and into the parking lot. Before he can follow, a hand stops him.

It's Silas.

He's lost his hat, and his hair is clotted with blood, but his face is whole. Whatever damage the bat did has already healed. He looks at me, eyes that swirl of oil-slick rainbow that I glimpsed before.

He says something to Willis, who throws back his head and roars. A sound that shakes the diner and rattles the windows in my car right behind me. But he doesn't follow us. Neither does Silas. He just watches.

My hip bumps the fender of my car. I blink. I don't remember crossing the parking lot. Neveah's sobbing and shouting at me to give her the keys. I can hear the song on the jukebox, just a tinny wail of a fiddle, leaking out the diner door.

And I realize that I don't want to go. Leaving means leaving Silas. If I drive away now, I know I'll never see him again.

"Neveah," I whisper, but she doesn't hear me over her own pleading. Louder, then. "Neveah!"

"What?!" she shouts back, breathless and terrified.

"I'm staying." I turn to her, let her see me. My conviction. My want.

"I'm staying," I repeat. "But you can go."

I throw her my keys. She reaches for them but misses and they clatter to the ground. With a sob she scrambles to find them and when she does, she wrenches the car door open and climbs into the driver's seat. I hear the locks engage, and then the engine, and she tears out of the parking lot, barely giving me time to move out of her way.

As soon as she's gone, I have second thoughts.

But I'm here, and Silas is there, just on the other side of the glass.

And I know what I have to do.

He waits for me to come to him.

I open the door, hands shaking. Dru's body lies still at my feet and Willis is panting like an angry animal, eyes trained on me. But I stay steady on Silas, remembering what he told me.

"I want you to leave," I say, voice barely above a whisper. It sounds pathetic to my own ears and I clear my throat and try again. "I want you and your Boys to go."

Silas tilts his head. The jukebox moves on to the next verse. And my heart breaks a little.

"Are you saying we're not welcome here anymore?"

I nod, even though it hurts.

"Well."

He bends to pick up his hat. Plants it firmly on his head.

"All you had to do was tell me so, Lukas." He gestures to Willis, who reaches down and, with inhuman strength, slings Dru's body up around his shoulders. Silas holds the door open and Willis goes through. Silas starts to follow, pauses to look back.

"But you owe me for Jasper," he says, voice hard like it wasn't before, "and I'll have to collect one day."

I watch them go. Watch until they fade into the darkness, until I'm sure there's nothing in the parking lot, not even racoons. And then I collapse.

Landry finds me on the floor the next morning and lectures me about alcohol and drinking too much. But we both know I don't drink and she makes me a stack of pancakes and an oversized cup of coffee. Workers come to haul the old jukebox away by noon, and we don't talk about it again. Neveah never comes back to the diner, and a few weeks later, Landry tells me that Neveah moved away, got into a four-year college somewhere. Jason and the Toad Twins wash up the next month, exsanguinated. Rumors circulate for a while about some weird drugs that must be on the market and their story even makes one of the primetime mystery shows, the connection to the Finleys' deaths too strange to ignore. The conspiracy podcasts go wild. They called it Murder in Blood River, and it causes a sensation for a while, but people have no idea. Not really.

Sometimes I hum that song, especially when I'm studying for my GED or getting the house ready for sale, but I never put my heart into it. I've decided to leave this shit town after all. Head to Dallas or Denver or something. Try to make my own way, see what happens.

I wonder if Silas will ever come to collect on Jasper's death, like he said he would. And I know all I have to do is sing for him and mean it, and I can find out. But I won't. Not for a while. Not until I'm ready. And while I wait, I'll dream of a beautiful black-haired boy in a cowboy hat with oil slicks for eyes.

WHITE HILLS

White Hills is everything Marissa ever wanted, right down to the welcome sign by the community mail drop reminding everyone of the HOA rules. Some people don't like HOAs, but Marissa loves them. They keep the houses looking nice and the people uniform, and isn't that one of the reasons she and Andrew chose to move here?

Well, that and its proximity to her in-laws.

And of course, the private golf course that Andrew spends most weekends on, and the no-children-allowed pool where she promised to meet her new friend Candy for drinks. (Only Candy never texted her back even though she sent a dozen *Hey Girl* texts with funny emojis, and even one pretty serious *RU OK?*)

Marissa pushes the uncomfortable thought of Candy's ghosting out of her mind and focuses on the positive as she pulls her BMW through the gate, tossing a wave to the security guard, admiring the way the afternoon sun catches on her new wedding ring, and then turning away as if he doesn't matter. But of course, it matters. What good are her accomplishments if there is no one there to bear witness?

Marissa has many accomplishments. Her body, for one. Tucked and toned and filled to perfection by the best professional surgeons, trainers, and estheticians Houston has to offer. Hair bleached to a stunning shade of summer. Hours spent on her social media accounts as a budding beauty influencer.

Some people think marrying well is not an accomplishment, but they never grew up poor outside of Chillicothe, Texas. Never slept four siblings to a queen size in an old two-bedroom house owned by their meemaw, never had to wear hand-me-downs to class or the same stupid pink blouse three years in a row for school pictures.

The memories fluster Marissa, and she adjusts her Gucci sunglasses as she clamps down on any emotion that might dare to ruin her perfect eyeliner. She tosses an expertly bleached lock of hair over her shoulder and gives the Bimmer some gas.

It's the baby, she thinks. Pregnancy makes women emotional. All the baby IG influencers say so.

She presses a freshly manicured hand to her newly bumping belly and smiles.

She hasn't told Andrew yet.

He's a good man, a really good man. But he's at a crucial crossroads in his career, and it's very important that the company see that he's CEO material. Part of that is a willingness to travel and work weekends and well, live and breathe the company. There's just no room for a child.

She understands.

But some men, well, some men don't think they want a baby until they see that little wrinkled face and those teeny feet and smell that distinct newborn smell, and then it all comes together.

Andrew will come together, Marissa's sure of it.

As long as it's a boy. She read that most women have boys first, anyway. It's nature's way of ensuring the man will stick around. She likes that, that nature has her own mind about things.

She pulls into their circular driveway, and now, looking up at their home, tears do come. Four bedrooms and three and a half baths at almost five thousand square feet. European white oak floors, Gaggenau appliances in the kitchen, separate his and hers walk-in closets.

Marissa was wrong when she said White Hills was all she ever wanted.

It is more. It is the dream.

All 4,914 square feet of their house is silent when Marissa walks in, her bright pink Manolo Blahniks tapping across the marble entry. The model furniture, even the fancy appliances she loves, is all as pristine as the day they moved in, mostly because Andrew is always working and Marissa doesn't make much of an impression on anything, even a house.

But that will change when the baby comes!

She can almost hear the toddler giggles, the pitapat of tiny shoes, the harried voice of the nanny.

Soon, baby, she thinks, and touches her hand to her belly. Wonders how best to work her angles for Instagram once she really starts to show.

Her iPhone dings with a text.

She eagerly digs through her Birkin and pulls out her phone.

It's from Andrew: *Meeting some fellas to watch the game at the club. Be home late. Don't wait up.*

Marissa's heart flutters, and her stomach drops.

She had planned to tell Andrew about the baby tonight. Was counting on it. But now, she's staring down another night alone, one she can't even mitigate with a bottle of Chardonnay (the baby, after all!).

Unless . . .

Marissa squares her shoulders. This is an opportunity, not a setback, and if there's anything life has taught Marissa it is that when God closes a door, he opens a window. She turns on her toe and marches right back to the car. She doesn't bother to wave at the guard on her way out (it's much more important to be seen arriving than leaving) and heads to the club.

She's mostly sure that Andrew loves surprises.

Dark mahogany and cigar smoke greet her as she makes her way from the tasteful lobby to one of four bars at the White Hills Country Club. The six-figure membership fee was a housewarming gift from her in-laws.

Her favorite part of the club is the upstairs patio bar designed in the Mediterranean style, the place where she met her new friend Candy, just last week. Candy was four hours into an afternoon of day drinking when the two women exchanged lipstick compliments over the bathroom vanity. Candy asked Marissa to join her, and Marissa would have never said yes except Andrew was off talking to the golf pro, and it had been two hours of Marissa sitting on an overstuffed chair waiting, her thighs sticking to the leather below her Lacoste skirt. So, when Candy slurred an invitation, Marissa accepted. Candy was tall and thin and although her roots were dark, she had that California girl aura about her. Or was it Florida?

That's it, she thinks to herself. *Candy's gone back to Florida. Only don't they have cell service in Florida?* Again, a bad feeling threatens, and Marissa quickly buries it.

She skips past the stairs that lead to boozed-out Tuscan fantasies and almost best friends. She follows the sound of football instead.

Marissa hesitates just inside the sports bar, momentarily blinded by the darkness. Small flatscreens cast illumination against the walls, and she's flustered by what the limited light reveals.

Heads. Mounted on the wall are heads. Deer, elk, even a water buffalo. And is that a wildebeest? Marissa thought those only existed in Disney movies.

Ball on the Washington twenty-yard line and it's fourth and inches. The Texans are going for it.

The words of the sports announcer barely register, but the groans of the dozen or so men into their high-end lagers and lowballs of liquor are the sounds of disappointment.

She recognizes Andrew's voice among them, a half-shout at the quarterback to DO SOMETHING, and beelines to the barstool where her husband sits, drink in hand. She touches his shoulder, and the smile he started with sours around the edges.

What a surprise and *did you get my voicemail* slur from his lips. He doesn't say *what are you doing here* but Marissa feels her violation, his contained outrage.

She drops her hand. Steps back from his unhappiness.

She almost has second thoughts.

But Marissa believes in maintaining a girlboss attitude that doesn't allow for second-guessing.

She lifts her chin and confirms that yes, yes, she got his message to stay home and not wait up, but can't a wife miss her husband and besides, she has some news.

Another groan from the crowd as their chosen football team blows it, and the guy next to Andrew, a heavier gray-haired business suit, curses crudely under his breath.

Marissa stands just to the side of Andrew's stool, hoping he'll offer her his seat. She makes a light comment about being on her feet all day (although she spent most of the day sitting in front of her laptop or in the manicurist's chair).

Andrew doesn't budge, but gray-haired suit slides over to make room for her. She accepts gratefully, giddy to be welcomed into this masculine domain. Only then does she notice the only other women in the room are waitstaff in low-cut blouses. She wonders if the wives of the club know about this place and decide they must. It's all kind of exciting, anyway. Men being men.

Andrew's absorbed in the game again, a hand now absently resting above her knee. Her confidence soars. She loves the weight of his fingers, the press of his wedding ring against her thigh. She's never been into sports, but she finds herself watching the TV anyway.

Another lost opportunity by the team, and the man next to her, the one who gave her his seat, jokes, "The team's been trash since they changed their name. Goddamn social justice warriors ruin everything."

Marissa doesn't follow sports, but she knows what he's talking about. She's seen people complaining about "The Chop" on TikTok, read an article about Indian mascots in *Vogue*. She raises her voice so everyone can hear. It's a declaration.

"I'm part Native American, and those mascots have never bothered me."

She realizes her mistake immediately.

She doesn't need to look to know that the gray-haired suit is staring at her, disgust curling his lips. She tries to laugh it off, backing toward the safety of her husband, but Andrew's eyes are wide, mouth hanging open, face red.

"I was only kidding," she ventures. "I'm not really—"

"Let's go." Andrew's hand, which had rested so nicely on her leg, is now pulling her roughly to her feet and dragging her out of the room, that ode to masculine violence with its animal heads and football games.

She trips, her heel catching on some unseen divot in the silk rug. She stumbles, feels the sharp pain in her ankle and knows she's going to fall.

"The baby!" She shouts it, unthinking.

Women lose pregnancies like this. Women fall and something breaks inside them and then there's only clotting and blood and and and . . .

She catches herself before she hits the floor. All that Pilates has given her a strong core and good reflexes.

Everyone's staring now. Andrew most of all.

She wants to rewind. This was not the way, not how she wanted to announce it.

But there's no going back. Only forward.

She straightens, ignoring the pain in her ankle. Touches a hand protectively to her midsection.

"I don't want to hurt the baby."

Later, in bed, Andrew simmers. It's a silent kind of rage, and something Marissa can usually fix with a well-timed application of oral sex, but now Andrew's spurned her advances and instead, he simmers.

Until he bursts.

"Why did you say that?" The words are a plaint, not anger, after all, but a soft kind of sadness.

"Say what?" She's rubbing La Mer cream on her hands, her legs tucked under Italian sheets.

"The part-Indian thing."

"I thought it might help."

"Is it true?"

Marissa hesitates. She has family stories, old pictures of browner-skinned ancestors. In high school, she joined the Native American Club.

Before she can answer, her phone dings. It's very late for anyone to text her.

"Who was it?"

She sets the phone down, feeling much better than she did moments ago. "Your mother. She texted to congratulate us on the baby. How did she know so fast? Someone at the club must have told her."

She thinks of the bartender, the waitress in the low-cut top, gray-haired suit.

She expects Andrew to smile back, but he only sighs, heavy and disconsolate, the sound of wind through bare branches. He leans over and kisses her on the forehead. It's a lingering kind of kiss. It almost feels like a goodbye.

"What's done is done," he says.

She doesn't understand what he means so she chooses to ignore it. "She's coming over tomorrow. We're going to brunch, and then to a baby specialist she knows."

Andrew sighs, his blue eyes immeasurably sad. "I thought you were French."

What a strange thing to say, but before she can respond, Andrew's turned out the lights.

Marissa tucks herself down into the sheets and pulls the Frette comforter up to her neck to stop the sudden shivers.

Elayne, Marissa's mother-in-law, is thirty minutes early. Her knock is crisp and precise, much like the woman herself. Elayne smells of Joy Baccarat and her Chanel suit is flawless. Pale silver hair gathers at her neck in a chic chignon. It would be crude to say Elayne looks like a million bucks because, surely, she looks like two million.

Marissa isn't ready. Hasn't had her decaf latte yet or finished drawing in her eyebrows. Without them she looks perpetually surprised, the top half of her face somehow missing altogether despite careful contouring around her nose and forehead.

Plus, she's wearing sweats—Rag & Bone cashmere, but Elayne eyes her hoodie like it's from the local mall. She taps her Rolex and reminds Marissa she pulled some strings to get her in to see this specialist today. The least her daughter-in-law could do is be ready to go.

"Marissa," Elayne says once they're in Elayne's Tesla and Marissa is suitably draped in Burberry silk georgette and linen. "Is that an ethnic name?" Elayne drives an electric. Not because she supports environmental causes, but because she owns stock in the company and once went on a yacht cruise with one of the Musk cousins. It's quite a concession, she tells people at parties, since her family comes from oil money.

"Hebrew, I think."

The Botox-smoothed corners of Elayne's mouth turn down.

"Or Latin."

They don't speak again until they arrive at the specialist's office downtown, although Marissa tries to engage her mother-in-law in conversation at least twice. Once about the traffic and then about Andrew's golf handicap. Both are equally prosaic fails, and by the time they pull off the freeway, Marissa is desperate to get out of the car.

The Houston skyscraper is a glass palace, an ode to a time when oil barons ruled this corner of the world. The weather has turned heavy, the promise of rain coming in off the Gulf.

On the elevator ride up, Marissa stares at the skyline. Thinks of Chillicothe, where the buildings never got higher than three stories, and the diner in College Station where she met Andrew after an Aggies football game. She told him she was a student there and that her parents had died, and she was living with an aunt. Only that last one was true, but she knew there was no way he was going to ask her out if she told the truth.

Sometimes lying is bad, but sometimes it's the only way to survive.

The nurses are all business smiles as they shuttle Marissa into a posh exam room. She can't fault the pale cream and stone decor in here. It reminds her of the spa at the St. Regis.

"I don't need to have a pelvic exam, do I?" she asks an attractive brunette with lips the color of sugar-free cranberry juice.

"Open wide."

The nurse swabs her mouth, says the specialist will be in to see her soon. She sits on the exam table, fully dressed, feet swinging off the end. Most doctors' offices have educational posters on the wall. Emergency numbers to call for mental health issues. She even had one doctor, a feminist-minded lady from India, who had a poster of how to do your own vaginal exam. She never went back to that one.

Here, there are drawings in frames, captured behind glass. Medical drawings. They look ancient, or at least old, like they belong in a museum, not this swank doctor's office.

Marissa hops off the exam table and moves closer. She sees now the drawings are diagrams. Human heads being measured and annotated, their features grossly exaggerated.

She can't quite read the cursive words, the unfamiliar numbers.

It reminds her of the sports club last night and her whole body shivers with a deep primal revulsion she doesn't quite understand. Part of her wants to look closer, comprehend what she's seeing, but another part of her wants to get as far away from the drawings as she can.

The knob on the door turns.

She covers her mouth to keep a scream in.

It's Elayne.

She's holding a smoothie. She eyes Marissa standing there with her hand over mouth and her eyes wide. She waits for her to shuffle back over to the examination table and sit.

She offers the smoothie to Marissa, which Marissa sniffs but doesn't accept.

"What's in this?" she asks.

Elayne, who is not used to being questioned, raises an eyebrow.

Marissa, who is not used to questioning, rushes her words. "It's just, I'm allergic to strawberries. All kinds, even the local kind, and the organic ones at Whole Foods. And I don't want, well, I have to be careful what I drink these days." She looks meaningfully down at her belly.

Elayne proffers the smoothie again, and this time Marissa takes it. Sips delicately from the metal straw, and that seems to placate Elayne. The drink does taste faintly of strawberries, but she's afraid to counter Elayne.

"The whole thing." Elayne's smile is brittle. "For the baby."

Marissa feels the hair on her neck rise. She wishes she hadn't come now, had begged off with a headache or morning sickness.

She sucks on the straw, the only sound in the room an embarrassingly loud, wet slurping, until the smoothie is mostly gone. Elayne gestures for her to finish it all, so she upends the glass and lets the last bit slush out across her lips.

She hands the empty glass back, her stomach feeling queasy.

She's pretty sure there were strawberries in there, and now she's worried about having a reaction. Last time her throat swelled, and hives broke out. She's worried, but at least she's in a doctor's office.

At least she thinks this is a doctor's office.

Elayne never actually said, did she?

Elayne sets the glass on the table beside her and roams to the window. The view is spectacular. The freeway glitters below.

"I'm not even mad," Elayne says, her gaze fixed on something in the distance. "Perhaps I should be. I mean, you lied to Andrew. To us. But then, I admire a bit of gold-digging ingenuity. I'm still not sure how you convinced Andrew to elope."

Now she turns, and Marissa feels small under her scrutiny.

"But 'part Native American'? I'm sorry. We can't abide that. And in a grandchild of mine? Well, do we know how dark the baby might be? How *savage* they might be?"

"But I'm white." Marissa holds out her pale arm as supporting evidence.

"Well, we certainly thought so. And there are white people who claim to be Indian all the time. I mean, old family stories, an enterprising relative who married an Indian for land rights. And I hear the Indians themselves say that kinship matters more than blood and isn't that quaint. I'm sure that's why they have blood quantum rules and ancestor rolls."

Marissa has no idea what blood quantum is. It sounds very technical, like dog breeding.

Elayne continues. "I hoped it was all a mistake, I truly did. But we checked."

Marissa remembers the mouth swab the nurse took. She thinks of the drawings on the wall.

"People say 'mutt' like a badge of honor," Elayne says. "What has the world come to when you can't be proud to be purebred?"

Marissa feels the first cramp just as Elayne trails off. She can't keep the small gasp of pain in, and as the next cramp rolls over her, her breath comes out in a moan. Elayne watches, silent.

"Oh!" Marissa clutches her belly.

"You're bleeding." Elayne's words are an observation. Her cool blue eyes track the spread of blood across Marissa's white pants.

Marissa doubles over, panic starting to clog her brain. *Focus,* she tells herself. *This can't be happening, this can't be happening, positive thoughts, manifest the life you want.*

"I'll get . . . someone." And Elayne is gone.

The floor is cool when Marissa lies her head against it, although she can't remember falling. She wonders where the nurse is, where the doctor is, where Elayne is. The smoothie glass sits watching, her only witness. That, and the heads in the drawings, dissected into brain size and nose and eye fold.

Another cramp rips through her. She screams. Begs. Tries to get to her feet and only ends up skidding in the mess of blood and . . . oh god.

The baby.

She vomits up bits of strawberry.

She thinks this is the worst of it, that this was somehow her fault, that this is all a mistake. She reminds herself that everything happens for a reason. Only she can't quite think of the reason for this.

Her lies, of course. And her outburst. And maybe she wasn't grateful enough in her gratitude journal. She babbles all this to Andrew as he drives her home from the specialist. She's wearing a borrowed skirt and underwear stuffed with the thick absorbent pads they give women after they've given birth, only there's not going to be a birth in Marissa's future.

She closes her eyes and lets the roll of the freeway distract her.

And the thing is, she begins to realize, Andrew knew. He knew when he left for work early, knew when Marissa prattled on about brunch with her mother-in-law and stroller shopping. Knew because he came to pick her up and had towels covering the passenger seat and didn't even act surprised or say he was sorry.

She tries to ask him about it, but all he says is, "I told you I didn't want kids."

"No, you didn't! You just said not now, not . . ."

She trails off at his look of pity, the way his lips press together as if she's embarrassing herself.

They pass through the gate of White Hills, around their circular driveway. She doesn't notice the guard on duty, forgets to read the HOA sign. Andrew helps her through the door, across the European oak floors and into the bathroom. She takes a very long bath that afterward she won't remember taking. She swallows down the Trazodone she keeps in the medicine cabinet. She curls up in her Italian sheets.

"I'm sorry," Andrew says.

She turns toward the wall.

"Mother will be here in the morning."

Marissa wants to scream WHAT FOR? She never wants to see Elayne again, never wants to be weighed and found wanting. And the worst part of all, the worst part is that she still cares what Elayne thinks. Wants to apologize, or explain, or claim innocence.

If she comes over tomorrow, you will have another chance to please her, Marissa thinks. And the shame of the thought burns through her like a lightning fire.

Marissa closes her eyes and doesn't answer.

Andrew's quiet so long that Marissa rolls over to face him, but he's not standing by the door anymore. He's gone. To the club or to sleep on the sofa or maybe even to a business meeting.

When she finally sleeps, all her dreams are of Indians.

Elayne arrives early again, but this time, Marissa's ready. She won't make that mistake again. She's freshly showered and styled, eyebrows perfect, pantsuit Balenciaga. She's made Earl Grey steamers and egg bites, and she's put them all out on the kitchen island.

She recites her mantras under her breath, the ones she posted this morning on her Instagram story. And most of all she smiles like nothing ever happened.

But she can't quite unclench her hand from the edge of the countertop.

Elayne slithers into the kitchen, once-overs the tea and tiny omelets, once-overs Marissa.

Marissa asks if she slept well, makes some banal comments about her own sleep. (*Slept like a baby* almost passes through her lips, but mercifully she stops herself.)

Elayne watches. Knows a performance for her benefit when she sees it. Says, "We're not quite done, you know."

Marissa holds on to her smile with all she has.

"There's the matter of your little bit of Indian blood. I would think a finger should do."

Marissa doesn't understand.

"Well, people say, 'part Native American,' but really, dear, what part? Your left side? Your right? And how can we get rid of that? But I have a compromise."

She reaches across the island and slides the chef's knife from the block. Places it between them.

"The pinkie should do. Cut that off, and we'll call it purged."

Marissa laughs because who wouldn't laugh in the face of a monster?

But the monster doesn't laugh back.

"I can take all this away, you know."

Marissa feels a tiny moment of triumph. "We didn't sign a prenup."

"I've already started the annulment paperwork."

"You bitch!" That comes out of Marissa's mouth before she can stop herself.

Elayne's sigh is an indulgence. "You're upset about the fetus, but honestly, what was that? A month? Two months? Barely a dream. You're young and fertile. If that's what you want, go have a half-breed baby with someone else. Just not here, and not with my son."

"But—"

"I'm offering you a way out if that's what you want. But look around you. The house, the car, the clothes on your back. It comes at a cost. You don't simply roll in here with your mixed-race blood and think you deserve all this permanently, do you?"

"Andrew—"

"—won't stop me, but I can take him, too." Her lips purse. "We both know you were a fling, but clever girl that you are, you convinced him to elope. But it won't last. The novelty will wear off, or you'll claim to have a headache one too many times, or open your silly mouth in front of his friends like you did at the club, and he'll want nothing more to do with you." Her smile is tight. "Men must sow their wild oats, but we won't be harvesting, dear. No, you're a passing interest, which I will tolerate for Andrew's sake, as long as you"—she points a finger at the blade between them—"know your place."

This is a test. Marissa understands now. And she sees that her pathetic breakfast and her trendy clothing was little more than an amateur's gambit. Here is the master setting out the knife. Here is where Marissa must decide what she truly wants, and what she is willing to do to get it.

"I think we can tear up those annulment papers, too. Come to a reasonable alimony agreement when the time comes."

Marissa stares at the pink polish on her perfect nails. She spies a chip she hadn't noticed before.

Elayne's sneering lips move, form a single word that seals her fate.

"Chillicothe."

Marissa looks up.

She slides off her shiny new wedding ring. Her manicured fingers wrap around the knife handle.

Everything for a reason. A door, a window. 100% girlboss.

No going back. Only forward.

She smiles at Elayne, and this time she means it.

"I want White Hills."

Elayne nods.

Marissa brings down the knife.

A BRIEF LESSON IN NATIVE AMERICAN ASTRONOMY

We were gonna be stars. That's what you got to understand. Big fucking stars. Like Jack and Rose or Mr. and Mrs. Carter, like our faces on every screen, dominating every media feed. Everyone already loved us, wanted to be us, wanted to fuck us. And people like that, people like us? Young, rich, famous? We don't just get sick and die. They've got med docs and implants and LongLife™ tech that keeps people alive for 150 years now if you can afford it, and we could afford it. So how could they let her die? How could I lose my perfect girl? How could they do that to me?

I keep the room dark. My agent's been calling but fuck him, you know? He says I'm missing important appearances, that if I'm not careful people will forget about me. Maybe it's time I move on, he says. Find a new girlfriend. Someone hot. Be seen with this new hot chick at a big premiere or something. They're launching a new luxury liner at the end of the week, he says, something that takes you to the edge of the atmosphere and projects your digital into outer space before hurling you back to the earth. A billion people will see your face, shining like an honest-to-God star. You should go, he says. Go to almost-space and smile a big almost-smile with a new almost-girlfriend and make people remember who you are. But who the fuck would want to ride that? You can't breathe up there. Who wants to go where you can't breathe?

My agent convinces the boss lady of DigImagine to come talk to me. She bangs on my door until I think she's gonna shatter the glass. That door cost me half my pay on that damn Japanese shampoo commercial where I had to wear that breechcloth and pose in front of a stuffed bison. Sure, it was humiliating, but I do have really stellar Indian hair—long, black, and it moves like it's got its own built-in wind machine, and the shampoo company was paying big for a few hours of easy work—flip, smolder, flip, smolder. It's what I do anyway most of the time, so why not?

Can't remember the last time I smiled for the camera. They want stoic, so I give them stoic. Cherie always thought it was funny. We'd laugh about stuff like that all the time.

Whatever.

Anyway, I don't want some motherfucker breaking my glass door, even if she is a studio head. I let her in because she's holding a little white envelope. I know that envelope. What it holds. That's the only reason I open the door. It's like I can already feel the wet burn on the back of my eyes. Only question is whose memories she's holding.

"I'm Carol Elder," she says, her bone-white pumps click-clacking on the hardwood as she strides through the door. "Sorry to hear about Charlene." She turns toward me and thrusts two things into my hands. The white envelope and an old-fashioned business card, her name printed in neat black ink on a white linen card. Our fingers touch briefly, accidentally, and hers are cold.

"Cherie." I tuck the card in the pocket of the bathrobe I'm wearing and take that envelope over to the kitchen island.

"What?"

"Her name was Cherie. Like the kind you eat. She was sweet." I don't know why I say that but it feels important, like she should get her name right and know she was a decent person. Despite all the other stuff, the rumors, the thing with the biowear executive. None of that mattered. She was good and didn't deserve to die.

Carol Elder follows me into the kitchen. She watches as I take a knife from the block and slice the envelope open. I catch her eyes roving the room. The overflowing ashtrays, the food cartons, the big engram needle on the coffee table surrounded by pieces of human hair, nails, flecks of skin. All laid out in a row. I swear she shudders.

"Did the doctors figure out what was wrong with her?" she asks. "What killed . . . I mean . . . why she died? Walked on," she adds hurriedly. "I mean, don't you people say 'walked on'?"

I can almost hear the roar of the Pacific out back, but with the blinds down and the air on, it sounds more like traffic on the 405. I don't give a shit either way. Cherie's the one who wanted to live on the beach. Malibu, she said. All the real stars live in Malibu, so we have to, too. Even if the truth is half the stars these days are kids with fancy digital setups in Kansas or big corporation simulations that aren't even fleshies. But Cherie wanted it, so we moved to Malibu.

I shake the contents of the white envelope out. A small glass vial, marked with the initials C.A., a little red band wound around the cap as a warning that the contents are high potency.

"Is this . . . ?" I say, suddenly breathless.

"We keep some high-grade engrams of all our big stars for . . . emergencies. Someone dies mid-production and a vial of quality engrams provides us with enough of the person to project a replicant that will get us through filming and retakes. Sometimes even a few promo interviews. Not in the flesh," she adds hastily. "We're not magicians. The replicant is digital, but it is interactive, and they look as good as the best simulations, but with more personality. Closer to the real thing." She smiles briefly. "We have some of yours, too, you know. It's part of your contract. DigImagine didn't just draw your blood when you signed with us for shits and giggles."

"I didn't think you did," I murmur absently, mind still on the vial in my hand. I'm afraid to ask, but I have to. "And this is . . . her?"

She nods. "She was under contract, but she wasn't actively filming anything for DigImagine, so her file is scheduled for decommission." She shifts her weight from one foot to the other. "The authorities can get excitable if we keep engrams when unnecessary. They usually go to next of kin but Cherie didn't list any. I thought you might want it. That it might help." She shrugs, her shoulders rising under her spotless pale silk suit, like she doesn't care either way. Just cleaning house, keeping things tidy.

My eyes dart to the coffee table, the needle. It's illegal to drop other people's memories directly into your brain, but I've been doing it. It's all I have left of her. Squeezing engrams off strands of hair left in her brush, fingernail clippings she liked to pile on the nightstand, sweat stains on the dirty clothes she left behind. It's fucked up. I get that. But she was my perfect girl. And then she died.

"There's a catch," she says. "If I give you these engrams, there's a catch."

"Anything."

"You signed contracts, Mr. Hunter. People paid you a lot of money to be in their digitals, and, well, you can't just not fulfill your obligations."

"Bereavement," I mutter. "Can't you tell them I'm taking time off for bereavement?"

"Yeah, I wish we could do that for you. I really do. But this is millions of dollars. The other actors, it wouldn't be fair to them." She leans in. I can see a hint of a tattoo on her shoulder where the blouse gapes at her neck. "And your community back home. Aren't they counting on you? Expecting you to represent them to the world?"

I wave that away. I don't think much about home anymore.

"There's talk of replacing you," she says.

I look up, annoyed. "With who?"

"The guy from Sixteen Tipis. You know the one." She gestures toward her short blond hair. I know what she means. He's got the wind machine hair.

"That guy ain't even Native. He's Persian."

"The engrams are yours, but you have two days. After that, it's out of my hands." She spreads her hands to show me just how powerless she is. But I know about Carol Elder. Rumor is she's a billionaire, controls the fate of every digital the studio puts out, and she's telling me it's out of her hands? Excuse me if I don't believe it. But here I am, anyway. An idiot who signed a contract and no way I can flip and smolder myself out of this one. And no way I'm letting them replace me.

The vial feels hot in my hand. She's in there, my girl. And we can be together again.

"Two days," Carol repeats. "That's all I can give you. Just you and her memories and then you're back to work, okay? Be grateful I got you this at all. Oh, and Mr. Hunter? Dez. I know you've been shooting scraps, but this is high-grade stuff. Don't put this stuff directly into your brain. Find a nice VR system and load them up in an Experience like a goddamn normal person. Nothing good will come from sharing brain space with a dead person, especially when it's biologicals."

"Yeah. Sure." But I'm already stumbling over to the table, my hand reaching for the needle, the vial with her initials whispering my name.

Carol opens her mouth, as if to protest, but settles for shaking her head disapprovingly. My hand closes around the cap, and I twist. It opens, and for the first time in days, I smile. I don't even notice when Carol leaves.

I wake up on the couch to someone knocking on my glass door.

"Cherie?" It takes me a minute to remember that it can't be her. My brain comes slouching back into my noggin and I see the engram needle on the table in front of me, Cherie's vial empty beside it. I reach for the vial, furious. Shake it, as if that's going to reveal something I can't see with my own eyes. But I'm a greedy bastard and I took it all and she's gone now. My chest hurts like my heart's gonna break in two and tears press against the back of my eyeballs.

I wipe at my leaky eyes and notice my video display is on. It's cycling through pictures. Sharp and technicolor. Cherie's audition reel. There she is, dressed as a Plains Indian maiden, her hair in two braids. Another as a prostitute, her hair in two braids. Another as an alcoholic mother, her hair in two braids.

I don't remember turning the display on, but I must have done it after I shot up the engrams, something to enhance the sensories. Looking at her, it's like I can still feel her in my brain.

The knock comes again.

I twist around to look at the door, but there's no one there. God, am I hearing things, too?

"I'm over here, babe."

I yelp at the sound of Cherie's voice coming from the kitchen. What in the entire fuck? But there she is, wearing her favorite shirt, blue jeans snug on her perfect ass. Her dark hair is twisted up in a bun on top of her head. She gives me a big smile.

"Good morning, gorgeous," she says. "I thought you were going to sleep forever. Want some coffee?"

I stare, slack-jawed. My heart speeds up, again, this time in that grasping desperation you feel when you wake up suddenly from a really great dream you don't want to let go.

"Are you . . . ?" I manage to stutter out.

"I'm alive in here," she says, tapping a pretty painted nail to her temple. "As long as my engrams are still floating around in your head, I'm here."

"That lady said they'd be potent."

"She was right. Coffee?"

We spend the morning together. A perfect morning. Drinking coffee and laughing over shared jokes. Jokes I thought died with her, but here she is, so real. Real enough to touch. And we touch. In fact, we touch until sometime in the late afternoon and the sun's starting to set somewhere out there over the ocean and I crawl out of our bed with nothing on and throw the curtains open wide so the ocean air comes in, and the dwindling daylight with it.

It's a mistake.

"Cherie . . . ?"

She looks up at me, catching the alarm in my voice. The flesh on half her face is missing, the sunlight degrading the memory of her to skeleton and ruin. I step back. I remember something on the news about engrams being sensitive to light, but I didn't know they would do that. For a fleeting moment, horror crawls up my spine and plants itself in my brain, right next to my true memories of my girl, fouling them. Turning them into something out of a B-grade screamer.

"Maybe we don't need the sunset after all," I tell her, my voice shaking as I hastily pull the curtains closed.

"Oh." She smiles as the light leaves the room. "Sure, Dez. We're better in the darkness anyway."

Dinner is a pack of cigarettes by shards of moonlight on the deck out back, the crash of the surf wild and rough in my ears. Cherie sits next to me, smiling. She's faded and eerie where the moonlight touches her face, but I try to ignore it. Keep my eyes out on the blackness of the Pacific. Even better, close my eyes so I can't see her at all, but can still know she's there.

But with my eyes closed, her scent is stronger and unnervingly sweet. So I open them.

She reaches over and lays her hand over mine. Something skitters over my fingers and I pull back. I swear I catch sight of a black beetle crawling over the edge of the deck and disappearing into the vast stretch of sand around us. But I'm not sure.

We are in bed, me and Cherie, and I wrap my arm around her. At first she is soft in all the right places, like I remember her. But then she is soft in the wrong places, flesh giving way where it should be firm. My fingers dip into the curve of her stomach and keep going, digging out flesh the same way the light cut away her face before, and the smell follows. I recognize it now, the startling stench of decay in my nose.

I gag. She turns toward me, sleepy and smiling faintly. Unaware that she is rotting and I can smell her doing it.

I stumble out of bed and into the bathroom, the contents of my stomach coming up. Shivers rake my shoulders and doubt settles in thick in my head. This can't be real. This is a fucking illusion, just like Cherie herself is an illusion. One I asked for, sure. One I want. Wanted.

I tiptoe back to my bedside and fumble in the dark for my phone. Slide the slim earpiece in. Find my bathrobe and pull the card out of the pocket where I left it. Recite the number into the voice recognition as I stagger out to the living room.

"Do you know what time it is?" Carol's voice comes in crisp and irritated just as her image pops up in my visual. She's sitting up in bed, in a dark room. A female shape sleeps beside her, hazy in the shadow.

I glance at the time output in the corner of the screen. "Five in the morning. Shit. Sorry."

She shakes her head, waving my apology away. "I was getting up soon anyway. What is it, Mr. Hunter?"

"I . . . I did what you told me not to do."

"And that is?"

"The engrams. Cherie's engrams. I injected them."

Carol's lips curl, her expression unsurprised and my confession unworthy of comment.

"And now she won't go away," I rush on. "And she's . . . degrading."

"What do you mean 'degrading'?"

"Like a corpse."

Carol makes a sound in her throat. "Jesus." She frowns. "Have you tried just sleeping them off?"

"You don't get it. She's here. She's real. She's in my bed right now. Rotting."

"You're simply hallucinating," she says, dismissive. "I warned you. You'll just have to wait it out."

"Dez, babe, is that you?" Cherie's voice from the bedroom.

Carol's chin lifts. "Is that her?"

I nod.

"I can hear her, too. It must have something to do with this." She taps her earpiece on the visual. "Amazing."

"You have to help me!"

"I'm not a memorologist," Carol snaps, sounding exasperated. I flinch at her tone, and she must take pity on me because she says, "I'll make some calls. See what I can do."

"Thank you."

"You're supposed to be back at DigImagine tomorrow."

Another day alone in the house with Cherie? Before it sounded like heaven, but now. "I'll come today if I can. But if she's still in my brain . . ."

"Will she follow you out of the house?"

Into the sunlight? "I don't know."

"Try that. And I'll try to find someone who can help."

I leave the house just as the sun is peaking over the eastern mountains. Out here in Malibu there's no paparazzi, no WeCams or fan drones that follow you around recording everything you do. The skies are patrolled, and the houses are behind gates. So it's just me, alone, as I slide into the back of the driverless car.

"DigImagine Studios in Culver City," I tell the onboard computer as the car comes to life.

"Good morning, gorgeous."

I grip the edge of the seat. Turn slowly to see her sitting next to me. She's wearing her favorite shirt, and those jeans. I stifle a whimper as she smiles, and I can see her jawbone through the place on her face where the rot has set in. See the hollow of her throat, grown black and green.

"Cherie?"

"You left without coffee. Don't you want your coffee?"

"How did you follow me?"

"I'm alive in here," she says, tapping a pretty painted nail to her temple. "As long as my engrams are still floating around in your head, I'm here."

"For how long?"

"Don't you want me around, Dez?" Her pout shifts to something else and she leans forward. Her eyeball looks wet and too round. "You promised you'd stay with me. 'Always,' you said. You said you'd never leave."

"I-I know," I stutter out. "And I meant it. But—"

"Always is forever, Dez." Her voice hardens. "Don't back out on me now."

"I won't." I tell the car to turn off and climb out of the back seat. Walk back to our house and through the glass door. Slump on the couch. The visual display is on. There's Cherie in her two braids. Cherie as a—

"Want some coffee, gorgeous?" Cherie calls brightly from the kitchen.

I wake up on the couch to someone knocking on my glass door. Light trails in as the sun rises over the Santa Monica Mountains in the east. Sunrise. Sunrise on the second day.

I look around, cautious. Everything is quiet. The visual display is off, even if I don't remember turning it off.

"Cherie?"

No answer, so I try again. Twist my neck to look in the kitchen, my breath in my teeth, half expecting her to be there, coffee in hand. But it's empty.

Relief bubbles up from my belly and I let my breath out with a harsh whoop. Carol Elder was right. I just needed to wait it out, sleep it off. The engrams must have worn off.

The knock comes again, and I pull myself up off the couch and double step it to the door, feeling clean and brand new. Carol's there, in another perfect suit, holding another white envelope. "We missed you at the studio this morning," she says, as she click-clacks over the threshold. "I did say two days."

"I tried," I explain, "but she was still in my head. She's gone now. Two days was the charm. And don't get me wrong, I'm glad I got to say goodbye. Grateful even," I say, folding my hands in prayer. "But we all gotta move on."

She stops and studies me, her chin tilting to the side. "I spoke to a friend of mine. A memorologist. She said that they've done experiments with test subjects willing to inject the engrams directly, and the results were . . . unpleasant."

"What does that mean?"

"The effect is permanent." Her voice is precise when she says it. I imagine she fires people with that voice. "The foreign engrams integrate into the subject's brains. They never go away, Dez."

I flip my hair over my shoulder and grin. Hold my arms out wide. I catch a glimpse of myself in the wall mirror. I look like a goddamn movie star. "Save your pity, Carol. Your memorologist is wrong. I'm fine. Better than fine. And listen. I learned my lesson. No more engrams for me, okay?" I tap my forehead to make my point.

She sets the white envelope with my name written on it on the kitchen island. "My friend said they have had some success countering the effect by reasserting the subject's own memories. Enough of Dez Hunter, and Cherie Agoyo is consumed."

"You're not listening to me. She's already gone." I feel a tinge of sorrow when I say it that way. I loved her. She was my perfect girl.

Carol presses a hand to the envelope. "Keep this anyway. A just-in-case."

"Fine, but I won't need them."

We walk back to the glass door. She pauses as she steps through. "I put them off one more day, but tomorrow is it. Be there tomorrow at six a.m. or you're in breach of contract and we call in Dabiri."

"I'll be there. No way Sixteen Tipis is getting my job."

She waves over her shoulder as she walks to her waiting car.

"Hey," I call. "Did you hear about that luxury liner that goes all the way to space? That's tonight. I might go. Be seen. Get my face projected into space!"

Yeah, that's what I'll do. And I'll look good doing it.

And I do. I condition the hair, find just the right outfit to wear, a mix between glam and effortlessly cool, and then let my good looks do the rest. My agent's more than happy to arrange to have a WeCam follow me, and my image streams out live to millions of households and handhelds as I wave and walk up the ramp onto the waiting liner. The party inside is thick with celebrities and I work the room, accepting condolences and welcome backs and propositions with equal charm. When I hit the bar, I almost order a champagne like I used to do for Cherie, but I catch myself and ask for some kind of Croatian beer instead that's all the rage.

Everyone gathers at the windows as we take off, and the acceleration through the atmosphere feels like nothing, smoother than the turbulence that used to accompany low-altitude flight. Soon enough we're approaching the hundred-kilometer mark and when the captain tells us we've reached the edge of the atmosphere, I lean forward and peer out the window into the perpetual darkness, like everyone else.

"Beautiful, isn't it?" Cherie says.

I swerve with a shout, my hand spasming. Drop my beer, which splashes the woman next to me. She cries out, and I rush to apologize, but she storms off, distraught, before the words are out. The WeCam over my shoulder buzzes as the viewer count erupts upward by a couple million.

"Smooth move, gorgeous." Cherie looks out the window not more than an arm's length away. She smiles, and worms fall from her mouth.

I reel back, slamming into the people behind me. I hear glass shatter and rough voices and someone pushes back, and I stumble forward. The WeCam buzzes loudly.

"I'm alive in here," she says, tapping a pretty painted nail to her temple. "As long as my engrams are still floating around in your head, I'm here."

I grip my jacket pocket, the one with the engram needle and the vial Carol Elder brought me. My just-in-case. They are solid and real under my hand, and I force my way through the crowd toward the privacy of the bathroom, my hand already pulling the needle from my pocket.

I stagger into the narrow space and slam the door shut. It catches the edge of the WeCam flying in over my shoulder, knocking it into the wall. The indicator light flashes an alarm, but I can still hear the buzz of view feeds growing. I splash my face with water, try to get my goddamn calm back, but when I look in the mirror, Cherie is right behind me.

I stifle a scream. Yank the vial marked D.H. free and twist the cap off with a jerk. Ram the plunger home and watch the needle fill.

Hands shaking, I dare to look up. Cherie hasn't moved. She's watching. But there's something dark in her face. Something waiting.

"Come on, come on," I mutter, until the needle is at full business and I grasp for the spot at the back of my neck and ram that thing into the injection spot. I can feel when the engrams hit my brain. Flashes of childhood. My grandma's place by the Rio Grande. My first ceremonial dance. And meeting Cherie in high school. And then my memories are all Cherie. Cherie at prom. Cherie when we both landed our first digital gigs. Cherie moving into the Malibu house. Cherie. Cherie. Cherie.

Carol Elder didn't tell me what to do if there is no Dez Hunter without Cherie Agoyo.

On the camera feedback screen I see myself, sweaty and panicked, my eyes glazed, and a needle gripped in my hand. And Cherie standing beside me, looking as real as any fleshie.

The WeCam dings, indicating the livestreams have hit capacity. A billion viewers, our faces projected across outer space.

We're goddamn stars.

FALLING BODIES

The insistent ding of the overhead comm wakes me from my slumber, and an artificial voice informs me that our passenger ship is approaching Long Reach Station. I surface from what was a pretty nice dream, wisps of a planet-side beach and a salty breeze lingering in my brain, and I do my best to stretch out the kinks in my back, the gift of my budget seat. There's still enough gate-jump sedatives floating around my system to shade the world in a hazy pastel of calm. I know it won't last, but right now, I like it. Nothing's too solid, no sharp edges. Complete opposite of reality.

I remind myself that getting to Long Reach means that the worst is over, that my planet and my problems are far, far away. I'm light-years from anyone who knows me. A billion-plus kilometers from the Genteel homeworld and anyone who might know what I've done—and who my father is. On Long Reach, I'll be just another college student, not the adopted son of a Genteel senator. Not some rich kid, and definitely not some failed social experiment.

This is a fresh start. A new beginning.

Isn't that what the judge promised when he sealed my records and commuted my sentence?

I press my forehead against my viewport, taking in the scene. Long Reach is a donut-shaped, silver-skinned behemoth rotating slowly around a tower axis. If the Streams are to be believed, it's the biggest artificial structure in known space. As I watch it turn, I remember speed out here is a lie: Long Reach is spinning at an almost unimaginable velocity.

That's the thing about space. Time and distance are nothing like they seem. A body's always farther away than you realize, always moving faster than you think. Out here, everything is an illusion.

Even me. Fresh-start college kid. What a crock.

But the funny thing about illusions is they're not all bad. Sometimes you need an illusion to keep your mind from cracking open against the truth.

"You look lost," a voice says from the aisle.

I look over to find a young woman smiling at me. She has a backpack hoisted over one shoulder and a cascade of cinnamon-colored curls over the other. I'm not an unattractive guy, but even with my new baby blues, this girl is way out of my league. A heart-shaped face, slightly tilted dark eyes, a figure under her school sweater that's hard not to notice.

"I only say that because you look like an Earther who's never seen a space station, is all." She says it nice, no implied insult like back home when one of the Senator's guests rakes me over and sneers "Earther" under their breath. "And I know all the Earther students on campus."

"I'm new," I say, liking the way it sounds, liking even more what it means. New like you don't recognize me. New like nobody knows me.

"I'm Krux." She thrusts her right hand forward, palm sideways. I know this greeting, so I offer my hand, too. Genteels don't touch hands upon meeting, so I didn't grow up with it, but I learned quick enough what people expected of someone who looks like me. It feels foreign, like mimicry, but there's something appealing about it, especially when Krux wraps her warm fingers around mine and shakes.

"I'm Ira," I say. An Earth name.

"Where are you from, back on Earth?" she asks. A little frown mars her brow. "Or did you grow up off-planet?"

So far off-planet I haven't stepped foot in this solar system since I was taken away as a child, but I don't tell her that. Instead, I have an answer, a ready lie for situations like this. Because Krux has made a mistake. I'm not who she thinks I am. I feel a little guilty about the lie, fresh start and all that, but I do it because it means she'll keep talking to me.

"The Americas," I say, knowing my answer is perfect. Vague, but good enough for small talk.

"Never been there," she says. She blushes. "I grew up off-planet. In a tank."

I smile. I like this girl who grew up on a ship but shakes hands like an Earther and is way out of my league.

The overhead comm dings again, and this time the voice instructs us to make sure we have all our belongings as disembarkation will begin in ninety seconds.

"Here." Krux tosses me a small holo, one of those cheap ones you can pick up at any Allbuy. I press my thumb to the holo and a video pops to life between us. Young people wearing traditional Earth clothes and greeting legislators on the steps of the Genteel capital. Another scene, Earther students serving meals to children in what looks like a refugee camp in some burned-out Earth city

I don't recognize. Another, Earthers old and young gathered in a circle, singing and dancing, smiles on wide faces, a banner in the background festooned with a blue and green planet and a red dove, obviously drawn by a child's hand.

The scenes are pretty mundane stuff, if a little heavy on the kumbaya propaganda, but there's something about that last one. The symbol on the banner.

The planet, the bird.

It takes a moment to click, it's so unexpected, but then it does, and my brain does a backdive and my hands start to shake. I smell blood, thick and pungent, I hear shouting, my vision sparks from pulse rifle flare.

I close my fist around the holo, hear it snap in my grip.

"Hey!" she cries.

"Is this a joke?" I growl from behind gritted teeth.

"It's a student org." She sounds more hurt than outraged. "The Student Coalition for Cross-Cultural Understanding. SCCCU."

Not terrorists, Ira. Not everyone's a fucking terrorist.

"Sorry," I say, my panic draining down a gravity well to leave me feeling like a fool. "It's the sedative," I offer weakly. "Brain's still foggy."

Her face softens. "Hey, why don't you come to our meeting tonight. Check it out. See what you think."

Despite my complete assholery, Krux is trying to be friendly. And what could a little student club hurt, especially one focused on cross-cultural understanding? I mean, aren't I the poster boy for that? Literally?

But Krux doesn't know anything about that, or about my father, the Senator. All she sees is my Earth face, and she thinks I'm just like her.

"We're meeting at seventeen station hour in the student commons. Come check us out. If you don't like it, you don't have to stay."

"Seventeen hour? Can't. I have plans." And I'm not sure if that makes me happy or sad.

She smiles, her dimple blossoming, again. "Maybe some other time, then."

The shuttle doors slide open, blowing in a wave of station air, that distinct mix of recycled oxygen, cold metal, and warm bodies. I turn to grab my duffel, thinking I should apologize to Krux, convince her to give me a tour of the campus or something, but by the time I turn back around, she's gone, swept away in the exiting crowd.

Long Reach Station is like nothing I've ever seen, and I spend my first few hours soaking it all in. Twenty levels of life, from engineering at the bottom through the single-digit levels of shopping and entertainment on through government offices and residential rings, and, at the top, the Genteel district. It's mostly humans and Genteel here, no surprise so near Earth, but there's a mix of other species, too. They always come with the Genteel, these other peoples from places they've conquered. Earth's not special.

I'd love to explore, ride the level lift up and down and gawk, but I've got a date, and not with the pretty girl I just met. So I catch the lift to level thirteen like my comm tells me and ask random strangers for directions until someone points me to probation services.

The digital nameplate on the door reads P.O. Mx. Stone, and my first impression is that "stone" is a fitting name for such a hardass. Hair razored to scalp, jaw like the aft of a battleship, obviously ex-military, and likely wishing they were back in deep space somewhere killing something instead of messing around with assholes like me.

Which is how they greet me when I walk in the door: "Sit, asshole."

I sit, taking in the room. Not much to it. One block in a sea of blocks. Standard-issue furniture that looks like castoff recycles patched to hell and back. A requisite inspirational poster on the wall. A clock set to station time and an Earth years calendar that doesn't apply out here in space but must be helpful when talking to the home office. Because Stone, to my surprise, is human, just like me. I wonder if that was the Senator's doing, finding me a P.O. from Earth. Thinking maybe that would make me feel at ease, get me to open up and relate. But all it does is make me remember . . . and that makes me nervous.

Stone has a comm tablet open in front of them and they're reading through what I assume is my file. They sound bored as they recite my life back to me.

"Orphaned on Earth, time in relocation services, adopted by a senator."

"A Genteel senator," I clarify, in case Stone is getting the wrong idea. "Not human."

Stone grunts, noncommittal, but I know better. Nobody likes seeing humans raised by their alien oppressors, unless you *are* the alien oppressor, and even then, I'm pretty controversial. My adoption was very public at the time, billed as a social experiment on all the Streams, PR'd as a "civilize the humans" kind of thing before I was whisked off to the Genteel home planet.

"Petty theft, truancy, expulsion from several schools."

Stone gives me the *poor little rich kid* glance, a millimeter short of an eyeroll, so maybe they don't give a shit about interspecies adoptions after all. But then they get to the rest of my file and lean back, their decades-old chair creaking under their weight. Eyebrows touch what would be a hairline if Stone had any hair, and then those battle eyes focus on me.

That's my cue to look at the wall, or the kitten-in-space inspo poster stuck to the peeling paint, or my fingernails. Anywhere but Stone's face. Because I'm pretty sure I know what I'll see there. The same thing I saw on the judge's face right before he sent me here. Shock, disgust, a little pity.

Stone swipes the comm closed and drops it on the desk. When they speak, I hear nothing but no-nonsense.

"I will remind you that you're on probation, so keep your nose clean. You are to attend classes, eat, sleep and shit in the dormitory, and limit any socializing to the hours between zero-six station and twenty station. Those hours are to be spent only on the university level where you will find everything you need. This next part should be obvious but let me make it clear: No drugs, no liquor, and no frequenting of any establishment where you couldn't take your mother."

I curl my lip, as if to say *What mother?*, because Stone must have already forgotten the orphan part.

Stone coughs over the misstep, but I know they read me.

"Understand?" they ask.

I nod. The Senator's keeping me on a short leash, but that was to be expected. Long Reach only *looks* like a fresh start, only *resembles* freedom. It's an illusion, just like everything else.

Stone says, "Check in with me weekly. You do that, we won't have a problem."

Another nod.

"I need a verbal."

"Sure."

We sit there, me not offering anything more, and Stone studying me. I can tell they want to ask, same as everyone else who has ever read my file. *Why'd you do it? How can you live with yourself?* And, always, *Why aren't you locked up in the bottom of some remote prison? How the fuck are you even here?*

I stand. "We done, then?"

They pass me an ID tag. I slap it against my wrist and it lights up, keyed to my DNA now. "That gets you to the levels you're cleared for. Nowhere else."

Great. Leash on and staked.

"Same time, same place next week, Ira. Now, get out."

Ira. Not asshole. I guess pity won, after all.

I give Mx. Stone a small salute and do as I'm told.

At first, everything's good. The Senator's collar chafes but it doesn't cut. My room in the dorm is a single. Decent. Bigger than my old jail cell, so I can't complain. My course load is average, most of the classes focused on science and math, subjects that kept me out of political talk and history, subjects where the Senator's name is unlikely to come up.

I spend my free time walking around the university level. I loiter in the library. I eat at the cafeteria, holding down a table by myself. Nobody bothers me, but nobody talks to me, either. Turns out it's easy to be back at my single in the dorm by twenty hour every night because I got nothing to do. I find myself looking forward to my weekly check-ins with Mx. Stone because at least it gets me off this level.

But in my third week of boring student life, the loneliness makes me reckless and I decide to do a little exploring. Nothing to get me in trouble. Just a walk, maybe dinner somewhere besides the cafeteria. I promise myself I'll be back at twenty station hour like I'm supposed to.

First, I try the residential levels thinking I'll stroll through some parks, gawk at some nice houses. I quickly find out my ID's not coded to let me in, just like Mx. Stone promised. But I'm undeterred and restless enough to keep trying. But it's no dice all the way down until I hit the single digits and then ping, I pour out onto level nine with the rest of the crowd.

I follow the flow of Earthers, Genteel, and others, letting the masses take me where they will. I shuffle down a street of neon and flash. It's mostly restaurants and shopping here, trendy eateries and midrange boutiques, Streams blasting the latest news and gossip from every open café door. At first, I worry I'll be recognized. Someone will see past the color job on the eyes and the new hair and see Senator K'lorna's adopted son. But after an hour not meriting even a second glance, I relax. It's nice, this anonymity, slipping and sliding through the throng like I'm one of them. Like I belong.

An illusion, but I'm all in.

I wander off the main thoroughfare and find a little hole-in-the-wall restaurant serving noodles with some kind of hydroponic vegetable and make a dinner of it. I sit in the front and people-watch.

It feels nice. Normal.

After a while, I decide it's time to head back. There's no day or night on a station, but they lower the artificial lights just like a sun cycle, so by the time I'm heading back toward the lift, it's dark, and I know it's late. The lifts run every thirty minutes, so if I catch the next one, I can be back at the dorm by curfew.

I'm standing, waiting, when a hand comes down on my shoulder.

It's so unexpected that for a second I panic, old memories shooting to the surface and gripping me by the throat. The smell of blood, the bark of a rifle, blood on—

"Ira?"

My heart pounds in my chest so loud it deafens me. Nobody's supposed to know me here. I can see it all slipping away. My new life, my reprieve, and I'm back under the Senator's thumb in front of the judge and there's no pity, only disgust.

And it's devastating in a way I never saw coming.

I whip around. I catch a dimpled smile, a cascade of cinnamon curls.

"It's Krux. Remember me?"

I exhale all that terror, my past trying hard to fuck me up.

"Are you okay?" she asks, face concerned, eyes wide as I suck in air too fast.

I manage to nod. "Startled me."

She gives me a look like I might be the biggest chickenshit in the system, but then says, "Hey, want to join us?"

The lift pings and the crowd pushes forward. We stand our ground, let the masses part around us, islands in the river.

"Us?"

Krux is with friends. Of course she is. Three other Earthers, the tallest looks familiar, like maybe he's in my quantum mechanics class. And there's a guy with the same cinnamon hair, the same tilted eyes. A relative, and he's giving me a look. Check that. That look means brother.

"You look like you could use a drink," she says.

Very astute, Krux. I could use about ten, the way my heart's pounding in my chest. But I promised Mx. Stone I'd keep my nose clean.

“One drink,” she insists, and the lift pings closed behind me.

Shit. Thirty minutes until the next. She squeezes my shoulder, but this time her touch is warm and nice and she’s showing me that dimple.

With the lift gone, there’s no way I’m making it back by twenty hour. I’m late, no matter how I play it. And now I’ve got thirty minutes to burn.

“Yeah. Sure. One drink.”

I expect to end up at some trendy club, the kind with kids on stims, loud thumping music, and watered bootleg. Or worse, some pretentious pub advertising artisanal brews and thirty credits for a reconstituted pretzel stick. But Krux leads us to some swank speakeasy tucked behind a corner Allbuy. The deco is all Earth, mosaics of green forests and blue oceans on the walls, furniture made of honest-to-God wood, or at least something that looks a lot like it. The air smells like rain, an artificial scent pumped in through the vents since, obviously, there’s no weather here. People dance to the smooth jazzy music, but they mostly drink, and the whole vibe does wonders to keep the panic I had earlier at bay. Despite breaking my probation, I’m glad I came.

Krux hands me a drink.

“What is this?”

“Mango. It’s a fruit from Earth, from the Americas, where you’re from. Well, a synth of it.”

“Nostalgia?” For a place she’s never been?

“Cultural pride. I try to keep alive the memory of how it was before the Genteel invasion to honor my ancestors.”

I remember her holo on the ship, her pitch for the student org promoting cross-cultural understanding. It makes me jittery and I'm not sure if I want to suck the concoction down in a single swallow or bolt while I can. She sees my indecision and asks, "What's wrong?"

"I'm not supposed to drink," I confess.

She tilts her head. "Why not?"

Because I'm on probation, and my current life is as fake as this mango, this wood, this rain. But that's too much to explain, so I drink instead. The drink is sweet and thick with a boozy kick that punches me in the face and tells me that I like it.

"Tell me about yourself, Ira," Krux says, sipping.

I shrug. "Not much to tell."

She tilts her head. "You look kind of familiar."

"I'm not," I assure her, but my pulse ticks up.

Her eyes narrow. "No, there's something . . ."

"Look at that," her brother says. His name is Ruck. He and their two friends are standing beside us at the bar.

We look. Walking in the door are four Genteels. Two female, two male. Human enough at first glance but it's the small things. The porcupine-quill-textured hair, the slightly longer limbs, the skin and eyes in colors that are just a little off from human. They're dressed in name brand fashions cut in nostalgic Earth styles, but otherwise they look like typical young people out for a good time.

"Don't they know this is an Earth club?" Ruck growls.

"Be cool," Krux warns, hand on her brother's arm.

I frown, wondering what happened to cross-cultural understanding. Wondering what they would think if they knew I grew up Genteel.

"They think they can treat us like trash but then they want to be us, wear our clothes. They claim Earth as their colony, force us to sign some one-sided peace treaty and now we're all friends?" Ruck's eyes are hard, angry. His gaze flashes to me, probably for backup.

"That's what happens when you're conquered," I say. It just slips out, nervousness making my mouth move before my brain does. I think Ruck's going to bite back, but instead he just stares, lips tight, something unreadable in his eyes.

"Let's dance," Krux says, then drags me to the dance floor. She pulls me close and wraps her hands around my neck. I slip mine around her waist. Our bodies move to the sensual beat, hips aligned, sweat building on my brow for more reasons than one.

She's quiet through the first song, happy to let our bodies handle the conversation, but as the next number starts, she leans in close to my ear. "Did you mean that?" she asks. "About us being conquered?"

I want to say no. Say I was just kidding, or I take it back, but the truth is I've seen enough to know that any protest to the contrary is just semantics. She can't see my collar, the leash, the illusion of who I am.

But if tell her all that, no way she'll stay here dancing with me.

So I kiss her to avoid saying anything at all. And she kisses me back, runs her hands into my hair and pulls my mouth to hers, and she tastes golden and bright.

"You know what, Ira," she says, mouth against mine. "Nobody can conquer you unless you let them. The real destruction happens inside you. As long as you're fighting, you're free."

I want to tell her I tried that and lost. So now I spin out, faster and farther than she can understand. Maximum velocity.

"Let's get out of here," I say, and she says yes.

I dream, and I'm back on the Genteel homeworld, Empyrean, in the Senator's house, a big dome-shaped mansion in the Genteel style.

There's someone knocking at the door, but the Senator's away, somewhere important, and I can't be bothered to answer it. But the door opens anyway—*blows* open—and into the foyer burst all these Earthers wearing combat gear and carrying pulse rifles. I stare, not only in shock, but because I haven't seen a human face besides my own in a decade.

A woman rushes toward me, big blue eyes like the oceans of Earth I've only read about in books. "We're here to rescue you," she says, and her mouth moves in slow motion.

I want to explain that I don't need rescue. This is my home. With the Senator. The only home I know. The only one I remember, at least.

But then a man is hoisting me up and throwing me over his shoulder like I'm not almost full grown, and we're running across the lawn and piling into a ship, and the Earthers are asking me questions and shouting about the Children of Earth and how they're going to take me home.

I know better.

Alarms have been triggered. Security is in pursuit.

But they're good, these Children of Earth. And they hide me away. One month, three months. The Streams are all abuzz with my kidnapping. The Senator goes on camera and warns the terrorists to bring me back or else. But the woman with the blue eyes tells me her name is Mariella. The tall man who carried me is José. There's also Abdul and Mia and Adelola. Their home, *my* home, is Earth. And as soon as it's safe, we'll all go home together, they promise.

I start to believe them. I start to want it, too.

So at month six when the Genteel soldiers break down the

Children's door, I pick up a rifle, and I shoot. But not at my abductors. All around me Genteel fall, some by my hand.

But so do Mariella and all the others.

And when the smoke clears and the Senator comes through the door, all I can think about is home. Not the dome-shaped mansion I grew up in, but the one I've never seen. That I never *will* see, now.

And so I shoot one last time.

Then someone's ripping the gun from my hands and shaking me so hard my brain rattles in my skull and there's a fist smashing against my cheek and I'm biting through my tongue and a tooth is flying loose and the bloodstained floor is coming up fast.

And the worst thing is, I deserve it.

I bolt awake, a scream on my lips. Someone's banging on my door, and it takes me a minute to realize I'm not back on Empyrean in the Senator's house. I'm a college student on Long Reach Station, and the voice yelling at me through the door isn't a Child of Earth but Krux's brother, asking if we're okay because he heard shouting.

I stumble naked out of bed, Krux's bed, and crack the door enough to apologize and assure him it was just a really shitty nightmare. He gives me a long look, but must finally decide I'm just a head case and lets it go.

Krux hasn't stirred. I check to make sure she's still breathing, then collect my clothes and dress. I'm on edge, both the lingering remnants of the nightmare and the guilt over blowing my curfew and ending up in Krux's bed setting in.

I check my comm, half expecting some angry message from Mx. Stone or, worse, the Senator, alerted by the ID tracker, wondering why I didn't make it back to the dorm last night. But there's nothing.

Still, it's best I get back.

Coward that I am, I decide not to wake Krux. I slip out the door, quiet as I can. I'm in a small pod apartment. There's a galley kitchen with a hot plate and a sink, a long bench that doubles as Ruck's bed and a sofa, and a small table.

Ruck is hunched over the table now, spooning hot cereal into his mouth. There's a screen on the wall opposite him and the morning Streams are running, talking heads vomiting up the news and gossip for popular consumption.

"Breakfast?" Ruck asks.

"Naw. I better go."

"You just gonna leave like that? After screwing my sister?" He pats the seat next to him.

He wants to talk, probably give me the speech about intentions and vaguely threaten to hurt me if I hurt her. I'm not volunteering, but I think I'd like to see Krux again, so I grab a bowl from the wash rack, scoop some of the cereal in from the pot on the hot plate, and join him. I've had some awkward meals, but this ranks up there as one of the worst.

He doesn't light into me like I thought he would. Instead, we both eat, our eyes fixed on the Streams. I've been good at avoiding them since That Day—and the Senator assured me he called in enough favors to keep the details off the Streams, but there's a knot in my chest as we watch, and I half expect the Genteel woman on the screen to mention my name and flash my picture at any moment.

"Ain't that some shit," Ruck says with a nod toward the screen. "Destroy our planet, force us to live in space while they steal our resources, and then hold a goddamn peace talk, like there's anything peaceful to say. Peace won't fix this."

I eat my cereal and focus on the Stream. Sure enough, they're talking about a summit on Long Reach Station. I hold my breath as the Genteel woman rattles off a list of dignitaries that will be attending. I can feel breakfast wanting to come back up as she says, her voice overly cheery, " . . . Senator K'lorna . . ."

"He's the worst of all of them," Ruck groans, gesturing toward the picture of the Senator on the screen. "Someone ought to shoot that shitbag."

Tried that, I think.

Ruck goes on for a while, ranting about Genteels and all that we lost on Earth. I let him, but the Senator's name is ringing in my ears, and all I can think about is maybe I'm more Genteel than human inside where it counts—and that if Ruck knew, he'd beat the shit out of me. Probably want me dead. If *Krux* knew, she definitely wouldn't have slept with me.

I mumble something about having an appointment, drop my half-eaten breakfast in the sink, and go. This time Ruck doesn't stop me.

There's a package propped up against my dorm room door. I scoop it up but don't open it until I'm inside and the door's locked. I check the return address, scared that it might give me away somehow, that the courier or one of my hall mates read it, and it said Senator K'lorna. But it's just some generic post locale, and I relax.

I tear it open to find an authorization ID tag and a holo. I click the holo on, and it shows me a map to a restaurant on level twenty, the time I'm supposed to be there flashing in green. It doesn't say it's from the Senator, but it's no coincidence I'd get authorization and an invitation to Genteel territory on the station on the day the Streams say the Senator's going to arrive.

I think about throwing the package away. Pretending like it

never arrived. But that's just delaying the inevitable. If I don't go, he'll track me down, and I'd rather meet him at some Genteel restaurant than have him on campus.

The clock says I've still got a few hours to burn, so I shower and dress, pick out the one Genteel-style suit I brought with me because he'll expect me to wear one. I carefully fix my hair and shine my shoes, and then I sit in my chair and watch the time pass.

The Senator didn't say anything, but I can feel in my bones the reason he's come. I look around my little room. Three weeks wasn't bad. Three weeks was the illusion of freedom, and it was good. I met a girl. I did okay in my classes. I kept my nose clean.

Maybe it was enough.

The restaurant is called Halcyon and it's up in the rarified air, all right. All the levels of the station I've been on before this have been metal creations, neon and pipes and circuits, whereas level twenty looks like Empyrean. Wide avenues of pockmarked calcified stone, manicured trees and lawns in shades of red and brown as if the entire world exists under a rusty sun. And under it all, the sharp smell of ammonia.

I take it all in with a feeling somewhere between homesick and bitter. Empyrean is the only home I've ever known, but I'm acutely aware it's not my true home. No matter what I do or who my adopted father is, I'll never truly belong. The Earther always shows through, and I can't decide if that's a good thing or not.

The Senator's there, already seated and waiting for me. The hostess is Genteel, lavender-skinned, her quill-like hair flat against her head, her watery amber eyes glaring suspiciously at me despite my Genteel clothes. I hand her my jacket and say nothing with my bland smile. She lets me pass.

The Senator's own suit is tailored and crisp, white hair tastefully styled. He stands when he sees me. I see his shoulder hitch and his sharp inhale. I think, *I did that.* But he covers the pain quickly and motions with his good arm to join him.

"Iraya," he greets me, and we sit. "It's good to see you."

"It's just Ira here."

The Senator's mint-green eyes crinkle.

"What?" I ask, already defensive.

"I wasn't questioning your judgment." A lie. He's *always* questioning my judgment. I wonder if he logs each instance of my questionable decision-making in a journal somewhere for the psychologists and sociologists to ponder one day when they talk about how my whole life, the Senator's whole experiment, was a failure.

"How is school?" he asks, moving on. This is the game we play where he pretends he's not checking up on me or reading Mx. Stone's reports, and I act like I have freedom.

"Good."

A waiter comes and relieves us of small talk while we order. The restaurant has real meat on the menu, not synthetic. It'll be the first meat I've had since I left Empyrean, so I order a steak, bloody. And, morbid sob story that I am, the blood makes me ask, "How's your shoulder?"

I say shoulder but that's just the euphemism we've agreed on, something that makes it sound less worse than the truth.

The Senator's smile is brief and pained. "Better every day. Genteel medicine is quite advanced. Better than Earth's."

According to the Senator, everything Genteel is better. But in this case, he's right. On Earth, he'd be dead.

The Senator says, "You didn't go back to the dorm last night."

Of course he knows. "I met a girl."

He perks up. "A Genteel girl?"

"Earth girl."

The Senator makes a disapproving sound. "Are you sure that's wise?"

We're both thinking of the Children of Earth. "Pretty sure I'm not gonna randomly hook up with another terrorist cell. My luck's not *that* bad." It's a joke, but I can hear Ruck bitching over the Stream in my mind, Krux telling me to fight. I clear my throat over the faux pas. "What are you doing here?"

"I'm staying next door in the hotel. This restaurant was convenient."

"No, I mean what are you doing *here*? On Long Reach?"

"There's a peace summit to work out some fine points of the new treaty."

"Why do the Genteel bother with this . . . *theater* when they've already won?" I mean it. It's not a flip question. I really want to know.

But he stares, as if he's trying to see inside me, like I'm acting ignorant on purpose. "We're not monsters," he says quietly. "There are factions on both sides that would rather see us at war, but the majority of both sides wants peace. *I* want peace."

I want to say that peace and subjugation aren't the same thing, but I know how that will sound, especially considering my past. *Our* past. I tell myself this is beyond my reach and not my problem.

"I saw you," I tell him. "On the Streams."

He grimaces. Starts to speak but the food arrives. He's quiet until the waiter's gone and the utensils are in our hands. I don't know what he was going to say before, but now he asks, "Did the Streams mention the Children?"

"Not yet."

"The editorial?"

"No."

When the Senator first adopted me, he wrote an editorial about adoption as a social experiment to prove that Genteel nurture can overcome violent human nature. Too bad it didn't work, and too bad his political enemies have never let him forget it.

He says, "You and I both know it's only a matter of time."

The red meat turns cold and hard in my stomach. I set my utensils down. Motion for the waiter and ask for something alcoholic.

"You know you're not supposed to be drinking."

"I do."

The waiter brings a bottle and two glasses. I fill one, drain it, and refill it. The Senator says nothing, just stares at me in that same questioning way, like he's trying to understand me but can't. The alcohol makes me feel better, and my hands have steadied.

Finally, he says, "We've been here before, Iraya. Your face on the Streams. You will get through this."

"It's Ira, and I just wish they'd leave me out of it." A child's complaint.

"It's too late for that."

I drink another gulp. The wine is quickly going to my head.

"If you're going to drink like that, finish your food."

I push the plate away with intention. "I'm not hungry."

The Senator laughs, but there's no warmth to it. "What college student isn't hungry?" He taps his knife against my plate. "This is real meat. Real vegetables. Do you know how expensive this is? How hard it is to get out here?"

"It's excessive. No one needs this." I'm thinking about what Ruck said about the Genteels. Thinking about my own duplicity. It's the shame making me act out. I've been through enough therapy to identify it, just not enough to do anything about it.

Then the Senator tells me why he's *really* here.

"The judge is revoking your probation."

I knew he was here to drag me home, but *this*? The shock sinks me down into my chair. I stare into the wineglass cupped between my palms, say the only thing that comes to mind as I struggle to process the news. "Because of the drinking?"

"It's political pressure. He's being accused of favoritism. There's a petition for his recall."

So nothing that I did. Just forces moving against me that I can't possibly control.

"No one knows I'm here," I say, and I know I sound pathetic. "I'm not enrolled as Iraya K'lorna, and there's no reason anyone would suspect I'm at this second-rate university on a space station. I mean, I changed my eyes, my hair. There's other Earthers here. I blend." *I could disappear if you let me. Pretend I was no one.* I don't say that last part, but it's implied.

His mint-green eyes darken. "I can't do that."

"Why not?"

Because you're a criminal, Iraya. You can't be trusted. He doesn't say his part, either, because he doesn't have to.

And all I can think is that this can't be real. But I know it is. Maybe the *only* real thing.

The Senator's done with his meal, and the waiter's there to clear our plates. I drain the bottle into my glass, drinking steadily until the check comes and the Senator's paid.

"I'll send someone to pick you up tomorrow evening once I've finished with my meetings." He stands, studies me. "On reconsideration, perhaps you should stay with me until we leave."

"I have a date." I don't, and I'm not even sure why I say it. I'm the asshole who left before Krux woke up, but I can't stomach the idea of leaving now with the Senator. Of this pretentious restaurant and this overpriced meal being my last gasp of freedom.

"The Earth girl? I'm not sure I like it."

"I don't care. You owe me this."

He frowns. *I owe you nothing. Any debt I owed you was forfeited after the Children.* I know he's thinking it, but all he says is "Iraya." He glances around to see if anyone is watching. We haven't made a scene yet, but he's a senator. Any scene will surely make the Streams. I don't see anyone watching us, but that doesn't mean we aren't being watched.

"A few hours," I say, my tone softer, less belligerent. "And then I'll go. Please."

Maybe he sees the shift in my body language, the flare of desperation in my tone. Maybe it's the *please* that convinces him to grant me this small freedom.

"Say your goodbyes tonight," he says. "But tomorrow, we leave." His hand moves, as if he might touch me, but he doesn't.

"I'm sorry," he says. "I tried."

I nod. What else can I do?

"I'm not trying to hurt you," he says.

I glance at his shoulder, the place near his heart where the bones have knitted but the scar remains. I'm not trying to hurt him, either, but neither of us seems able to stop.

I end up back at Krux's pod after all, banging on the door, asking her to let me in. I'm not even sure she's there, but I can't go back to my dorm, knowing that after tonight I'll be sleeping in a jail cell.

She opens the door and I fall inside, half-drunk and fully spinning. I confess what I can, careful not to mention names but telling her about my controlling father, my collar and leash, my desire to be free but with no idea how to make it a reality.

She gets me to the bench, gives me a glass of water, and comms Ruck. He arrives quickly from somewhere nearby and they confer out of earshot. I can only hear their mumbling argument, but already I feel like a fool. I barely know this girl and her brother. Why would they help me? Why would they care?

I push myself to my feet, ready to make my excuses and leave, certain I'll never see either of them again once I'm out the door.

Krux stops me, pushes me back onto the bench. Ruck sits on my other side.

"Maybe SCCCU can help," she says.

It takes me a moment to decipher the acronym, and then I remember her sales pitch on the ship. "Your student org? The cross-cultural understanding thing?"

Her eyes slide over to Ruck. "I might not have been entirely honest about that."

I can feel the planetary shift, the recycled air going stale. It's suddenly hard to breathe as this particular illusion shatters.

"There is no student org, is there?" My voice is flat, a ghost tumbling through space. "That red dove on the banner. You're Children."

And now my stupid joke about joining another terrorist cell hammers me to silence. Of course this girl that's way out of my league doesn't really like me. Of course it was no coincidence we met on that ship or in front of the lift.

"We can get you out," she says, grasping my hands. "If you do something for us."

I look up, hope sparking like the light of a distant star.

Ruck's voice is a knife. "Take out the Senator."

And just like that I'm reminded that stars are dead.

Krux must see the refusal in my face because she says, "You shot him before."

And I *failed*. Don't you get that? I tried to kill him and I failed. And he doesn't even hate me for it. He's *forgiven* me for fuck's sake. That's the worst part. He won't even let me have the horror of it, only the shame.

"No."

Krux gets up and goes to the kitchen. She squats down to pull something from beneath the sink and comes back. She sets a metal box on the table between us.

"You won't have to shoot him this time." She says it quietly, like blowing him up is better. More civilized. "You activate it here." She points to an indentation on the side of the box. "After that, all you have to do is give it to the Senator. Tell him not to open it until he's alone, that it's a gift. Something personal."

"He doesn't trust me."

"You're his son."

"The son that shot him!"

"He thinks you were brainwashed, right? Influenced by those months you spent with the Children. This is different."

"How is this different? You want me to kill my father."

"He's not your father," Ruck shouts. "He's a fucking Genteel! He stole you as a baby. Used you in his propaganda crusades. Erased your cultural heritage. Why are you loyal to that man?"

"Ira." Krux touches my shoulder. "Do you want out or not? Freedom is right there. It's right there. All you have to do is fight for it."

"This isn't about my freedom," I say, knowing the truth of it. "This is about revenge. Revenge for those dead Children."

"It's about both," she says.

"And you can benefit from it," Ruck adds, "or you can stay on your leash."

"You don't understand."

"I do understand," he barks, rising to stand over me. "I understand better than you think. And I'm starting to think maybe you like wearing that collar. Maybe being on that leash ain't so bad for you. As long as you can live in a fine house and eat real meat. As long as the Senator's always there to bail you out. Maybe being a social experiment isn't so bad. Maybe you've decided being one of them is fine by you."

"Fuck you!" I rise and swing for his face and connect, but he recovers fast and barrels into me. Krux is screaming as we crash into a table and knock over a shelf, plates breaking around us in the tiny space. He gets a good punch in, but I hit back, and then Krux is pulling him off me, and I'm lying on my back panting, trying to catch my breath, head spinning with wine and rage and fear.

"Coward," he spits before he stomps into the bedroom and slams the door.

I lay there wondering if he's right. Is that my problem? I'm just a coward?

The court-appointed therapist asked me why I shot my father. Was it an accident? Had I aligned my loyalties with my kidnappers, a common enough syndrome? Or was it something else?

I could have lied, told her I didn't mean to shoot or that the Children had messed with my brain. But I'd been looking right at the Senator when I pulled that trigger, his mint-green eyes locked into mine. And all I'd felt was rage. A rage so deep and foundational that I couldn't look at it without going blind. He glimpsed it, too. In that moment. I know he did.

But it didn't last, that rage. It morphed into horror, then guilt, then regret, and then, finally, shame. It became something lodged in my heart, real as any gunshot, bleeding me out in increments.

Krux comes to me, squats down beside me, and hands me a cold medipack. I press it to my smarting jaw.

"Do you love him?" she asks.

Love and hate. Is there a difference? Not for me.

When I don't answer, she tries, "You don't remember anything about Earth?"

She wants me to. It would be easier if I did. Easier if I hated the Senator and remembered my first home, but I've never been easy.

"Tell me something, Ira. Make me understand."

I close my eyes, sure I don't owe her that.

"Mariella was our mother," she says.

Mariella with the ocean eyes. "She was kind to me." I don't know why I say it, but I want her to know. "And Ruck is wrong. There's no mansion for me. I'm going back to prison." I want her to know that, too.

"Then helping us is your only way out."

She goes back to the table. Picks up the box and holds it out.

I don't know how long she stands there, arm extended. Or how long I stare. Time and distance in space is a lie.

Finally, I take the box. "What do I have to do?"

Krux smiles, but it's sad, strained. "I'll get Ruck and we'll go over the plan," she says, voice quiet. "You're going to see Earth again, Ira. We all are. We're going home, and you'll finally be free."

I spend the night with Krux although I don't know why since I know who and what she is, except that maybe I don't want to be alone. We go over the plans. Once, twice, again and again until Ruck is satisfied that I understand how it's going to go.

"There are others helping us," he explains. "Our job was simply to secure your cooperation. They'll have a new ID for you, transportation off Long Reach, and a place you can disappear after this. Somewhere to start fresh."

Start fresh. Already tried that. It didn't work.

Last thing he does is give me a gun. "Only use it in case of an emergency," he says. "Better to go with the box." What he doesn't say is that I had a gun once before and wasn't able to get the job done, so they're not convinced I'd be able to do it this time, either.

In the morning, I go back to my dorm. I stop at an Allbuy along the way. There's a Stream running on the screen behind the register and images flash across it. Genteel and humans, the peace summit. And there: what I've expected all along.

Senator K'lorna and his son, Iraya K'lorna. Ungrateful adopted son who tragically turned against his father and joined an Earther terrorist organization. When the cell was found, a half dozen Genteel soldiers were killed and the Senator himself was shot. Iraya K'lorna was sentenced to prison for his role in the shooting, but no one knows where. There are rumors that the Senator has hidden him away and is helping him evade justice. And now the presiding judge is demanding a review of the case.

I hunch my shoulders, try to avoid eye contact with the man behind the register, and pay for my holo. I sneak into the dorm through the back way, sure that my hall mates have seen my face on the Streams by now. It's only a matter of time until someone figures out it's me and gets the courage to knock on my door.

I shower and sleep a bit. I pack, leaving the place neat and clean, saying goodbye to something that was barely mine to begin with.

I don't wait for whoever the Senator's hired to come retrieve me. Instead, I use the twenty-level clearance tag to go to the Senator's hotel next to the Halcyon. It's big and posh, taking up the entire vertical span of the ring. Inside, I politely ask for the Senator's room, inform the desk person to tell him that his son is here to see him.

I see the way she eyes me, knows who I am, may even be a little scared of me. But she comms up, and the Senator instructs her to tell security to allow me to pass unharrassed. I can't hear their conversation, but I can tell there's some debate. I'm dangerous, after all. Untrustworthy. I should at least be searched.

I start sweating, Ruck's gun tucked into my waistband and digging into my spine.

But the Senator's adamant, no doubt worried that security will rough me up, terrorist that I am, but, finally, the big man with the rifle lets me pass with no more than a disgusted glare.

I keep sweating all the way up the lift. Remind myself this is the only way out. Forward motion, no going back.

I press the comm at the door and it dings softly. For a moment I think of the ship that brought me here. It feels like a lifetime ago, time so unreliable.

"Enter," he calls, and the door slides open.

The room is huge, four times the size of Krux and Ruck's pod, maybe more. There's a separate bedroom and bathroom, a receiving area, a relaxation pit, and there, a desk where the Senator sits.

He looks up as I enter. "Iraya. I said I'd send someone."

"I thought I'd come myself."

A line furrows his brow like he's not sure what to think, and I realize he's as uncomfortable with me as I am with him. And in that moment I know I've reached terminal velocity.

I hold up the package to show him. "I got you something."

He pushes the chair back and stands but doesn't approach. "That seems unnecessary."

I step forward and set it on the edge of the desk.

He stares at the box. "Listen, Iraya."

I pause.

There are things the Senator could say right now that might change the trajectory of our lives. Throw us out of each other's orbit. But he's always been the planet and me, the moon. Only one of us is circling the other, and everyone knows moons never escape their gravitational parent without a catastrophic event.

The Senator says, "You should have commed before you came."

I exhale all hope for a different trajectory. I turn and am almost at the door when I hear it.

The click of the metal box opening.

I bow my head. Of course he couldn't wait, couldn't even give me that.

I pull the gun from my waistband. In case of an emergency.

"What's this?" he asks, head down as he peers into the box. "A holo?"

He presses the holo and it comes to life. I know what's on it. I recorded it before I came. But I listen to it anyway. Listen to his breathing shift as my words hit him. Harder than any homemade bomb.

"Iraya?" He sounds angry, but I know that it's fear. "What's going on?"

"It's what I said on the holo, Dad." I never call him dad. Only Senator. But this time, I allow myself the indulgence. This one last time. "I used to think I would be happy if only I hadn't been adopted. Then I thought I'd be happy if I could only get to Earth. But Earth's no more my home than Empyrean. And nobody can give me a home, not you, not the Children."

It was Krux who made me realize it. Going on about Earth and how wonderful it would be when she was a tank kid, born and raised. Her Earth isn't real. It's an illusion just like everything else. But I don't need illusions anymore.

I'm already cracked wide open.

"All I want now is to be free from this fucked-up narrative, nobody's political pawn. But you can't give me that either. So I've decided to free myself."

I raise the gun. I can see the memory of the last time we were here like this together flash across his face, darken his eyes.

The Senator lifts his hands, a surrender come too late. "Ira, no!"

Time and distance are nothing like they seem. A body's always farther away than you realize, always moving faster than you think. In life, everything is an illusion.

Even me.

"Last time I shot the wrong person," I say. "This time I won't."

I put the barrel in my mouth.

I pull the trigger.

EYE & TOOTH

First class ain't what it used to be, so it's not like you're missing out.

That's the lie Zelda tells herself as she shifts in her economy middle seat trying to get comfortable. The stranger on her right is sleeping, big snores dribbling from an open mouth showcasing some seriously subpar dental work, and her brother, Atticus, has claimed the aisle seat. She doesn't begrudge Atticus the space to stretch out. Six-foot-four needs the legroom.

She watches the flight attendant move through the promised land up front, offering rows one through three single servings of protein cookies and snack bags of baked pea pods. Baked pea pods! What kind of shit is that?

When she and Atticus used to fly first class, they were always getting a real meal with cutlery and everything. Not that she could eat it, but it was the thought that counted. The respect.

Used to be their line of work was appreciated. Used to be when a client called begging for a little supernatural wetwork, a hunter could demand pretty much anything they wanted. Rich fucks would break the bank for someone with Zelda's and Atticus's talents to save them from whatever awful horror they'd conjured up.

There was this one time this golf pro out in Temecula shot his ex-wife, but she refused to die. He'd panicked, put another half dozen holes in her like he was Rambo, but she kept getting back up—some real ghoul shit. The man had called the hotline sobbing, ready to confess all and turn himself in to the police if only his ex would stop *wriggling*.

Zelda had handled that like the professional she was. Talked the man down, told him they'd be there by nightfall and to just keep his old lady locked up until she and Atticus could arrive.

He'd paid for first class.

But in the end, it hadn't mattered, because the dumb bastard hadn't listened. Instead of waiting for the professionals, he'd tried some bullshit internet remedy that said throwing salt at a corpse would keep it down, when every true hunter knows it's grave dirt or nothing. Got his face eaten for the effort.

But face-eaters aren't the usual in their line of work. Most monsters are run-of-the-mill. Haints that needed settling, river spirits that some greedy land developer riled up. Once, a poltergeist that was terrorizing some poor condo board.

And while some TikToking amateur had led the Temecula golf pro astray, most of the time the internet got it depressingly right. Seems like more and more these days, people rid themselves of the supernatural on their own. Weekend warriors with flamethrowers, AKs, and some basic YouTube skills were making the art of monster hunting passé.

It used to be a finesse business that required a special skill set.

Now it was all do-it-yourselfers.

"We there yet?" Atticus asks, slipping off his headphones.

On cue, the overhead crackles, and the flight attendant informs them that the plane is beginning its descent.

Atticus winks at his sister like he saw that coming. Maybe he did. He's always been able to see things others can't. Mama calls it the Eye. Says what Atticus has got is hereditary, that there's always been someone every generation in the Credit family blessed with gifts that help them fight the evils of this world. After all, monsters ain't new.

"You remember to make the car rental reservation?" Atticus asks. "And the hotel?"

"Yes to both. You know I never slack."

"I know, sis." He says it with affection. "Where we at again?"

This is Atticus too. Can't be bothered to remember where they are even though it says Dallas on his ticket, same as Zelda's. Mama said it's because he's living in two worlds most of the time, Ours and Theirs, and people like that aren't so good with mundane things like eating three squares and remembering where the fuck they are, so that's Zelda's job. Take care of her little brother, handle the details, and be the Tooth to Atticus's Eye.

Because Seeing ain't the only power that runs in the family. And where there's light, there's also got to be some dark.

The plane cuts through low clouds and the rumble of thunder. The ticket says Dallas, but their destination is really somewhere west of Fort Worth. Soon, Zelda's steering an F-150 into a sky streaked the color of old blood by the setting sun. Streetlights flicker to life just as the dark clouds blister and break, rain hammering the roof of the truck. An endless line of eighteen-wheelers sends wave after wave of tsunamis against the windshield, turning visibility to shit, but the big rigs thin out as they leave the sprawling suburbs. It's full dark outside by the time Zelda picks up a rural route that cuts through some of the flattest, emptiest land she's ever seen.

Under the steady thump of rain, the GPS leads them deep into cow country. The road winds through a series of one-traffic-light towns, each as full of the dead and dying as any graveyard. She squints down poorly lit side streets looking for speed traps and bad cops, but all she spies are dilapidated storefronts and neon-signed dollar stores.

Another hour and Zelda's pulling the truck up a long dirt road, tires rolling over dips and drops deep enough to rattle her teeth. A burst of lightning fires up the night sky, edging a big old farmhouse in a halo of light. Their destination looks like it was plucked from an old painting, maybe that one with the girl in the field reaching for something she ain't never gonna get.

The house has three stories of gray wooden planks, a peaked roof, and a columned porch. Another flash illuminates a yellow cornfield and a hill of derelict farm tools. Zelda's pretty sure she spots the rusted-out frame of an old tractor out there, too.

"This is some real *Children of the Corn* shit," she mutters, thinking between the storm and the dark and the absolute lack of anything good, they've stumbled into her own personal nightmare. She's a California girl, preferring a hot sun and streets thick with prefabs over this nothing and nowhere. "Why'd we take this job again?"

"Living ain't free," Atticus says.

"Neither is dying."

Her brother chuckles, his voice a deep rumble that twins the thunder. He rouses himself enough to look around. As his posture sharpens, so does his whole being, like he's coming into focus, like that laconic man-child on the plane was all surface, and he's peeling it back inch by inch as they get closer to whatever's waiting for them in that big old house.

"You feel anything?" Zelda asks, already tense, happy that Atticus is here to do the seeing, knowing she'll be the one to do the biting.

"Not sure. Could be." He gives his sister a look. "Or it could be your energy interfering. Maybe after we meet the client, you take a walk and give me a little space."

Zelda eyes the dark stretch of empty, the persistent rain.

Atticus grins. "Unless you're afraid there's nobody out here to hear you scream."

Zelda huffs. "Now, why would you say that?"

"It's the truth."

"The truth is overrated."

"'Death ain't free' . . . 'the truth is overrated' . . ." He shakes his head in mock disappointment. "If I didn't know any better, I'd say you're shook."

And then he's out of the truck, long legs halfway up the farmhouse steps before Zelda's even closed her mouth. She hurries after him, hoodie pulled tight against the weather, feet slipping across the muddy path. By the time she joins her brother at the front door, he's got his hand out, knocking.

They don't wait but a second before the door swings open. Dark eyes look Zelda over. She's suddenly aware of how sorry she must appear with her frizzy hair and mud-splattered sweats.

"Ms. Washington?" Zelda hazards.

Unlike Zelda, their client is immaculate, her hair freshly pressed, her red dress, designer, looking like this treacherous weather wouldn't dare touch her.

"You were supposed to be here two hours ago," she says.

"Drive was longer than expected," Zelda apologizes. "And the rain."

"I've got supper on the table." Washington's voice is crisp and no-nonsense, the Texas showing through only in the drop of her *r*s. "Take off those wet jackets first and leave them here. And watch your shoes. I don't want mud in this house."

Zelda does her best to shake off the outside before Washington leads them through the foyer and directly into the dining room. On the table sits a pot of red beans, a thin layer of congealed fat resting on top, but the cornbread in a metal pan is golden and smells of butter. Even if Zelda did eat things like beans and bread, she'd decline, but Atticus doesn't hesitate. Six-foot-four stays hungry, and she's never known her brother to turn down a free meal.

Washington watches Atticus fill a plate, a small, satisfied smile curling her lips. Maybe it's only the woman taking pride in her cooking, but something about it is enough to raise Zelda's hackles. Washington senses her looking, her *judging*, and, cool as can be, raises a questioning eyebrow.

Zelda's a professional and has no intention of insulting the woman in her own home when they're here to do a job and get paid, so she smiles and looks away.

And sees dolls.

Everywhere, dolls. In a bookcase, in a custom cabinet, on the mantel. Most are porcelain, but there's a handful of paper dolls captured behind glass and some ancient-looking vinyl dolls with jointed limbs arranged in various poses beside them. There's even a shelf of corncob dolls in gingham dresses and woven hats like Grandma Credit used to have.

"You a collector?" Zelda asks, trying for polite. The painted faces staring back at her are unsettling, and she can't quite suppress the shiver that works its way down her back. Big bad monster hunter, but she remembers that Lumberjack Laura job, the child-sized ax and the all-too-adult-sized bodies. After that, nobody could blame her for not liking dolls.

"I'm a creator, not a collector. There's a difference." Washington sounds mildly insulted. She pulls out a menthol cigarette from a green hard pack and lights it. "You can have a look if you want."

There's a tap of feet and a little girl comes trundling into the room. She's not more than six, maybe seven, with braided pigtails and cat-print leggings. She's wearing one of those old-fashioned boots with a metal brace that makes her drag her foot, but that doesn't stop her from beelining to Washington. She peers out at Zelda from behind the older woman's chair.

Zelda waves. The girl, shy, waves back.

"What'd I tell you about guests," Washington says, voice sharp with disapproval as she hauls the girl forward and shakes her by her chubby arms. "Go on, and don't come out until I say so."

The girl ducks her head and limps back the way she came.

"She didn't mean nothing," Zelda says, the cruelty making her blood heat, her teeth ache.

Washington exhales a cool plume of smoke. "I know you mean well, but that child's got to learn. So, don't tell me how to do my job, and I won't tell you how to do yours." She stretches her mouth in a smile she doesn't mean, white teeth and gums showing.

Silence hovers in the room, thick as the fog wafting from Washington's menthol. The only sound is the click of Atticus's fork against his plate. Zelda, thinking of the money, thinking of professionalism, says nothing. She hates herself a little for it, though.

Finally, Washington speaks. "Granny told me about your family.

Real deal Black folks. Root workers and hoodoo queens. My granny worked with herbs, made tonics for the folks around here, but it wasn't anything like what you got. They say there's *power* in y'all's blood." She exhales. "You sure you won't eat?"

"No, ma'am. I'm sure."

Washington's eyes narrow. Cigarette ash floats down to the table like poisonous snow. "They say one of you got the Eye. It better be true, after all the money I'm paying you."

Zelda clears her throat. "Speaking of money."

Washington reaches into the sweetheart neckline of her dress and pulls out a fat envelope. She waves it in Zelda's direction before tucking it away. "When you're done helping me," she says.

"Actually, you were vague on the phone about exactly what kind of help you needed."

"You got the Eye. Why don't you tell me?"

Zelda shares a look with her brother.

Washington turns to Atticus. "Oh, it's you that has it. Tell me what you See."

Atticus pauses with his fork halfway to his mouth. He straightens and his gaze goes soft. But only for a moment before he glances at Zelda and shakes his head.

"It doesn't work that way," Zelda hedges. "Maybe if you just told us."

Washington grunts, eyes lingering on Atticus. "Out in the cornfield. That's where I first found the birds. I thought it was just an old possum gone feral or something, but it progressed."

"Progressed?"

"Got the barn cat next, and then . . . something bigger. I hear it sometimes at night, out there screaming."

"Screaming? You sure it isn't a fox or a cougar?"

Her eyes go flat. "Too big for a fox, and there haven't been cougars in this part of Texas for fifty years."

"Too big? So you saw it?"

Washington rubs another dusting of ash from the table. "Something's out there."

"Then I best go take a look." Zelda's thinking that as much as she doesn't want to go out in that cornfield, especially at night in the middle of God's own storm, her absence will give Atticus the space to do his Seeing.

"You look tired, young man." Washington stubs out her cigarette. "I got you a bed ready upstairs."

Zelda's taken aback. "I don't think—"

"At least let him rest here while you hunt around. Besides, the only motel in town's got bedbugs."

Zelda looks at Atticus, who yawns big, eyes drooping. He does look tired, maybe even a little wan, and Zelda knows he's got a sensitive nature.

"All right," she concedes. "While I hunt."

Washington leads them up creaky stairs to the guest bedroom. It's not much to look at. The floral wallpaper is starting to yellow and floorboards creak around thin oval rugs. A knitted blanket is folded neatly at the foot of each of the two narrow beds, and Zelda can clearly hear the rain knocking against the roof.

"You going out there?" Washington nods toward the curtained window.

"Yes, ma'am. It's what you hired us for, and I won't let a bit of rain slow me d—"

"Don't track mud in," she says. "I don't want to have to clean up tomorrow."

She walks away, leaving Zelda with her mouth open. She stands there for a moment, stunned at the rudeness, wondering why she's trying so hard when Washington is giving her nothing but attitude back.

"She's a piece of work," she mutters.

She turns to Atticus. He's already curled up on the bed, the thin blanket not even long enough to cover his feet. Zelda frowns, worry for her little brother replacing her irritation.

"You okay?"

"Sick," he mumbles.

"You shouldn't have eaten those beans," she says, thinking of that layer of fat.

"Trying to be polite."

"Trying to feed your stomach." She shakes her head. "You See anything down there?"

"Doll," Atticus murmurs.

"Creepy as fuck, right?" Zelda can tell that without the Eye. "I couldn't live with all those little eyes staring at me, but maybe that's countryfolk. Maybe they're different."

Lightning crackles outside and Zelda goes to the window. She pulls back the curtain and peers out over the cornfield.

She sucks in a breath.

Something *is* out there. Something low, moving on all fours. Another flash of lightning, and . . . nothing. But she was sure she saw . . . She shakes her head. Probably a fox.

"I'm going out," she says over her shoulder. "Washington's keeping secrets, and I don't like the way she talked to that child. Can you look around while I'm . . . Atticus?"

But the only answer she receives is the soft sound of her brother's snores.

—

It's wet and miserable, and Zelda wishes she hadn't come out after all. She's a city girl at heart, and this pitch-dark country shit is worse than a horde of zombies running through the Fashion Place Mall.

It takes her a moment, slick fingers sliding over the switch, but she manages to flick on her flashlight. She aims it low. The amber beam lands on a face.

"Shit!" Zelda shouts and stumbles back.

But it's only the little girl, the one from dinner. She's standing there in the rain, her back to the field, big black eyes on Zelda. Her clothes are soaked through, shoulders limp in the downpour.

"What are you doing out here?" Zelda hisses, still working to calm her heartbeat. "You oughta be inside, out of this rain. You're gonna catch your death!"

The girl stares, mouth a wide pink O.

"Your grandma's gonna tan your hide when she finds out you're out here," Zelda chides, and immediately regrets it, thinking of how Washington scolded the child earlier. How the older woman riled up that something inside Zelda that made her hot, loose, less in control. She's not sending the girl back to that.

The girl motions Zelda forward.

Zelda gets a feeling. She doesn't get feelings often. That's Atticus's game. But sometimes even a Tooth can tell something's wrong.

"You got a name?" she asks the girl.

Nothing. Maybe she doesn't talk.

Zelda sighs. She knows it's dumb to bring the kid along, maybe even dangerous. But she's also got a feeling this kid ain't just a kid, like she knows something. Maybe something she can't say but can show.

Zelda glances back at the house one last time before she slips off her hoodie and wraps it around the child. She zips it up, pulls the strings snug, and gives the kid a smile. "Well, come on, then, No Name. Maybe you can help me out."

She lets the girl lead her out into the cornfield, her little form limping along. They go deep into the high stalks until she can't see the house. Can't hear nothing, either, beyond the steady pounding of rain battering the dried-out husks. But then she smells something. Something dead.

The kid stops. Zelda thinks maybe she smells it too.

The kid points.

Zelda trains her flashlight where she's shown and squats down, the girl hovering over her shoulder. Zelda nudges the lump. Turns the thing over. She's not sure what she's looking at beyond a mess of flesh and fur, white bones poking out every which way. It steams slightly, still hot despite the rain.

Zelda swallows, can't quite stop herself from licking her lips.

"Hungry," the kid whispers beside her.

Zelda near about jumps out of her skin. It takes her a moment to collect herself, to turn to the girl and mutter, "So you *can* talk."

But the girl stays focused on the dead thing in front of them.

"Yeah," Zelda says, once she realizes nothing else is forthcoming. "Something was hungry all right, but we must have interrupted its meal." Which means it could still be close.

Zelda stands. Listens. But she can't hear anything but rain, and the scent of death is so overpowering she can't track past it. She's not going to find anything out here tonight.

"Let's get you back inside," she says. She keeps the kid beside her as they retrace their steps. She's halfway convinced Washington is wrong and it's just some kind of natural predator out here in the field, but she keeps her head on a swivel, her senses alert, just in case.

As they pass out of the field and back to the yard, she feels eyes on her and looks down to find the kid staring. "Go on, then," she urges, gesturing toward the porch. "Go get dry, and don't tell your grandma you were out here with me. She's like to skin us both."

The kid slips out of Zelda's hoodie and solemnly hands it back before she hobbles off to the house. Zelda spares one last glance for the field before she follows. The lights are all out, the little girl disappearing into the shadows as quickly as she had appeared out in the field.

Zelda tiptoes up the stairs and quietly pushes the bedroom door open.

"Atticus," she calls softly. He's where she left him, curled on his side. She decides to let him sleep. Plenty of time to catch whatever it is tomorrow.

Zelda dreams of hunting, of freshly torn flesh and blood in her mouth. She opens her eyes, slowly, carefully, half expecting to find herself curled up to a fresh carcass. Her phone says it's almost dawn despite the lack of light coming in the windows, and she can still hear that damned rain. She thinks about trying to go back to sleep, but her stomach's rumbling and more dreams will only make it worse.

She decides to hit the hardware store she spotted on the way in before the house wakes up. Buy some wood and wire and set a few traps. Catch whatever's out there feeding in the cornfield to placate Ms. Washington, get paid, and get the hell home.

The ride back to town takes the better part of an hour but she's at the local True Value when the door opens. She grabs a cart and makes the rounds, pulling what she needs off the shelves. She gets to the cashier and he smiles at her. He's old enough to be her father, but his oiled hair and the strong odor of aftershave tell her he's a flirt. She wonders who the hell there is to impress out here and realizes that today it's her.

"Haven't seen you around here before," he says, not even trying to hide his enthusiasm.

"Visiting."

"Yeah? Where at?"

She considers ignoring the question but decides she might as well do some fishing. If she's wrong and it's not just a critter, it would be good to know what she can about Ms. Washington. More times than not, whatever's troubling a place has to do with the people occupying it.

"Ms. Washington. She a ways outside town."

"Ah, sure I know her. Dolores and I went to school together."

"Dolores." So that's her name.

He sighs, heavy. "That family's had more than its fair share of heartbreak."

"How so?"

He leans in, the chance to gossip with a newcomer obviously too tempting to pass up. "Her father died under mysterious circumstances, if you know what I mean. Sheriff said he passed away in his sleep, but everyone knows he beat her mama, and when her grandmother found out?"

"Murdered." Zelda remembers what Dolores said about her grandmother and her tonics. She can't help but smile. Her own mama's told her about how back in the day women would take care of bad men when the law turned a blind eye.

The man spreads his hands. "It's ancient history now, and Dolores never let none of that stop her. She became something. Somebody. Traveled all over the world with those dolls of hers. Put our little county on the map." He points his thumb to a wall of pictures just over his shoulder. Zelda spots a handful of local celebrities smiling in faded Kodachrome: the mayor at a ribbon cutting in front of a candy store, the local football team holding up a trophy, a beauty queen waving from a hay float. And sure enough, there's Dolores Washington posing with one of those corncob dolls, only this one's as big as a real child, blue ribbon pinned to its chest.

"Now she lives out there in that house all alone," he says.

"Well, she's got her daughter." *Granddaughter,* she amends in her head. The girl's too young to be her daughter.

"Her daughter don't talk to her no more. Not since the accident. Hate to say it, but she blamed Dolores for what happened."

Zelda doesn't follow.

"The granddaughter." The cashier lowers his voice. "She was playing out in the cornfield and stepped on some kind of old animal trap. Snapped closed, took her foot clean off." His hand mimes the bite of metal jaws. "By the time they found her she'd bled out. Couldn't keep enough blood in her to keep her alive."

Zelda stares.

He purses his lips before he brightens. "I'm glad to see Dolores has got some company now. Can't imagine how hard it must be to be all alone, nothing to keep you company but a bunch of old dolls."

Zelda's back in the truck and speeding down the road, her shopping cart left behind. She doesn't need to build a critter trap. She knows who and what the monster is. Can't believe she didn't put it together when it was all right there in front of her. If Atticus had been awake, he'd have Seen something. Or maybe he had.

Doll, he'd said. Only she hadn't understood.

And then he'd been too tired, or too sick, or—

"Oh God."

Power in the blood. That's what Washington had wanted, what had made her eyes linger on Atticus, what had curled her lip in satisfaction. Because Lord knows your dead grandchild can't survive on birds and barn cats. She needed what all revenants need: a person to feed on, and even better if it's someone with power, someone like Atticus.

Zelda slams the gas down harder and sends the truck jumping forward, sliding on the slick street. The tail end tries to fishtail, but she rights the thing, tires spinning, as she curses herself and prays she's not too late.

"Atticus!" she screams as she barrels through the door. She takes the stairs two at a time and throws herself against the bedroom door. It rattles in its frame, locked, and holds. She focuses, calls some of that heat that's always waiting down inside her, and slams into the door again. This time it gives.

And there's the little girl, the little *doll,* curled up next to Atticus. He looks to be sleeping, but there's a looseness about his limbs that speaks of something more than sleep, that shouts at her that if she doesn't do something, he's never waking up.

The child looks up, heavy-lidded. Blood crusts her little mouth, streaks Atticus's neck and shoulders where she's been feeding. Her boot brace is off, and she's missing her leg below the knee, corn husks sticking out along the cuff of the fabric.

"Hungry," she whispers.

Zelda starts to move. To do what, she doesn't know. To rip the girl away from her brother, to open her own vein and feed Atticus her blood, hoping to replace his? But she doesn't take a step before her back catches on fire.

She stumbles, howling in pain. Her hand grasps desperately for whatever weapon has pierced her between her shoulder blades, but she can't reach it. She hears something in her body pop as she stretches, and then she catches a glimpse. Protruding from her flesh is a jumbo-sized wooden knitting needle half as thick as her wrist.

"I will not lose my grandchild!" Washington cries as Zelda staggers around to face her. Gone is the cool, put-together woman with the pressed hair and the perfect dress. The woman before her is wild-eyed, desperate. Determined.

"You can't have my brother!" Zelda grinds out between clenched teeth.

But Dolores doesn't hear her, gaze focused on the girl, on Atticus as he lies there dying. "Your family's got that old blood," she half whispers. "*Magic.* If anything can make my baby alive again, it's that."

"The magic runs two ways," Zelda hisses.

Dolores turns, stares.

"Your granny should have told you that magic always comes in twos. Light and Dark." Zelda spits blood, grins through the pain. "Eye & Tooth."

She calls her power, some of the same power that runs in Atticus's veins, only hers is bent different. She lets it bubble up, become appetite. Her fangs descend, her nails sharpen. Zelda roars as she reaches back and rips the needle from her flesh. The pain is clarifying, almost exhilarating. She rolls her shoulder, pops the bone back into the socket, and tosses the needle aside.

Washington screams, raises her hands as if she can ward off what's next. But it's too late for that, and Zelda's been hungry too.

The rain has finally stopped and there's a cool breeze blowing in through the open windows when Atticus walks down the stairs, headphones around his neck. There's a thick bandage around his throat, white gauze crisscrossing his shoulder. His steps are a little slower, skin a little chalkier, as whatever poison Dolores put in those beans works its way out of his system.

"You ready to leave?" Zelda asks.

"More than ready." He eyes the phone cradled against Zelda's cheek. "Who you talking to?"

"On hold with the airline."

Atticus's gaze flickers to the girl. She's sitting next to Zelda playing with a paper doll.

"I can't just leave her here," Zelda says. She fingers the blood-stained envelope and the splayed-out twenties on the table. She knows it's not much, but she figures it's just enough to buy an extra ticket in economy. "And I told her no eating until we're home and I can teach her how to hunt proper."

Atticus grunts, noncommittal, and slides on his headphones. "I'll wait in the truck."

Zelda knows he's not happy, but he won't make a fuss, because he understands, just like Zelda, that sometimes the best monster hunters are monsters themselves.

RIVER OF BONES

A SIXTH WORLD STORY

CHAPTER 1

"You've got mail, Kai," Maggie announces as she comes through the front door of her trailer.

I'm sitting on her second favorite chair doing nothing. I meant to peel some potatoes for dinner, but I sort of lost track of time. Something I'm prone to lately. Whole days can go by while I sit here staring at the cheap wallpaper and melting into the well-worn sofa cushions, the passage of time no more than a concept with which I'm not particularly familiar. She's been letting me crash with her since Glen Canyon.

Ah, I know what you're thinking. Crashing? At Maggie's? *With Maggie?* But it's not like that. She sleeps in the only bedroom, and I toss restlessly on the old broken couch thinking about dying. Not in some intangible existential way, but in a *hey I remember what it's like to struggle to breathe as your heart slowly ticks down to nothing* way.

Do I sound bitter? Ungrateful? I'm not. It's my choice. All of it. Even the dying. And I'm pretty sure that if I asked, she'd welcome me into her bed. It's just . . . "What did you say?"

"Someone sent you a letter." She waves a sky-blue envelope in my direction, the back bearing a wax seal marked with a series of wavy lines and the silhouette of a castle turret on a mountainside.

We don't get much mail. I mean, there's no federal government anymore and the tribal council's not sending bills and junk mail. So a letter is out of the ordinary, and the one Maggie's holding, well, it's more than unusual. Because I recognize that shade of blue, that water and castle sigil, and my heart thumps hard in my chest. The room goes a little hazy as adrenaline hits my veins. I swallow around it. Make myself breathe through a spike of fear.

I keep my expression smooth, my voice casual, and ask, "Who from?"

Maggie shrugs and flops down in her favorite chair. Tosses me the envelope, which lands in my lap.

"Doesn't say. But it's got your name on it."

And so it does: *Kai Arviso* scrolls across the front in ornate black script.

"So the question," Maggie drawls, "is who can afford fancy paper like that, and why would they bother to send you a letter all the way from the Burque?" Her eyes narrow as she kicks her feet up on the coffee table. "It is from the Burque, isn't it?"

"Who delivered it?" I ask, stalling as I try to get my brain working, really not wanting to break that telltale seal. Because I know exactly who sent it.

"Ben brought it over," she says. "Said it arrived at the All-American with a shipment." She grins a little and her whole face lights up, no doubt remembering something Ben said. It's one of my favorite things, and something Maggie doesn't know about herself. When she smiles, which, granted, is rare, it's a beautiful thing. A thing worth living for.

But before her smile has even begun to fade, my brain replaces it with another look. The one she gave me on Black Mesa right before she pulled the trigger. The last thing I saw before I . . . Well, you know.

I push back that memory and clear my throat. "Where's Ben?" I ask. "Is she not coming inside?"

"She said she couldn't stay. Grace has her out running errands and she didn't want to be late getting back. But we'll see her at the All-American's grand reopening."

"When's that, again?"

Her look is quizzical. "Next week. We've been planning it for weeks."

"Yeah, of course."

She lifts her chin in my direction. "Open it, Kai," she says, reading me, despite my best efforts not to let losing my shit be so apparent. "No use putting it off. Unless you already know what it is."

"That obvious?"

"Yeah."

"I don't know what it says." I turn the envelope over, the sharp corners biting into the flesh of my now shaking hands. "But I do know who sent it."

She tilts her head, curious.

I run a fingernail under the seal, splitting it open. Draw out the thick paper and read the note, confirming what I already knew.

"It's from my ex."

Lachryma Urioste was my first serious girlfriend. I met her in a place I wasn't supposed to be. A masked gala I was definitely not invited to in the private hacienda of one of the most powerful families of the Burque. Hers.

The Uriostes are one of the old families of the region who trace their lineage back to the Spanish invaders of the 1500s. Those early settler families always had an outsized influence over the politics of New Mexico when it was a state, and after the Big Water they parlayed their place in local politics into something even more powerful. When the federal and state governments fell, along with their handmaidens the multinational corporations, La Familia Antigua stepped in. They became the political and social power of what was left of the city of Albuquerque, a new kind of Burqueño royalty in our post-apocalyptic world, unchecked and rarely questioned. And me, Navajo son of a shamed college professor and a missing and presumed dead mother, made the mistake of loving one of their princesses.

It did not end well.

"I met their queen, you know," Maggie says. "Elena Urioste." She's got her big knife out and is cleaning her nails. The rest of her arsenal is spread across the coffee table. A sure sign she's bothered, but on a scale of irritated to murderous, she's only annoyed. Cleaning her weapons is one of her tells that I've become attuned to. I don't think she does it on purpose. Maybe she doesn't even realize she's doing it. But that's just Maggie. Scary as shit even when she's not trying. I guess I should be glad she didn't decide to clean her guns. Then I'd be in trouble.

"You mentioned it," I say.

"At that horror show called Knifetown. She was there at the auction where they tried to sell Ben. Don't know what she was planning to buy—body organs, a slave—but she talked to Rissa about making trade inroads into Dinétah. I told her to fuck off."

"Of course you did." Only Maggie would talk back to Elena Urioste and not fear retribution. She's braver than me.

"So what does her daughter . . . your ex . . . want, Kai?"

"She wants me to come to the Burque."

Her hands stop. "Yeah?" Her voice is deceptively soft. "Maybe you better read the letter aloud."

There are few things I want to do less, but:

Dearest Kai,

I know an apology will never be enough to make amends for what happened between us, but please know that I regret that day and what transpired thereafter with every fiber of my being. Not a day goes by that I do not wish things had been different between us, and so it is with some feeble hope that you feel the same, or at least harbor some fair thought of me despite my unworthiness, that I write to you to ask for your help. You have no reason to render me aid, no reason at all. But know that I would not ask if my circumstances were not dire. You are the only one who can save me now. If you do not, I fear that in a fortnight I will be as good as dead.

The woman who once held your heart,
Lala

Maggie pulls one of her guns from its holster and starts taking it apart. *Click* goes the release, *clunk* goes the cylinder. She pulls a soft rag, an old toothbrush, and a vial of lubricant from a leather bag.

"Lala?"

"It's a nickname."

She glances up. "One you gave her?"

I shake my head, remembering how I once told Maggie that girls like nicknames. Knowing she's wondering if that's some line I recycled on her.

"Family nickname," I clarify.

"Didn't she almost have you killed?" She swirls the toothbrush through the barrel. "She makes it sound like you just had a bad breakup."

"Yeah." I exhale. "It's starting to feel like a pattern. Girlfriends trying to kill me."

She winces, and I regret saying anything. I may not be able to move past dying, but she's just as guilt ridden about being the one that killed me.

"Lala lives in her own world," I explain, my gaze drifting to Maggie's gun. Wondering if that's the same one she shot me with.

Maggie's hands keep moving, and she doesn't look at me. "Are you going?"

"To the Burque?"

She nods.

"It's probably a trap."

"What if it's not?"

"And she's really in danger?" I shrug and hope it's convincingly nonchalant. Because despite everything that happened, I am thinking the same thing. But I say, "I don't owe her anything."

Maggie's silent for a minute, the only sound the *swish, swish* of the brush against metal.

"You once told me that she was just a hookup. That you didn't love her."

Nothing I hate more than my own words coming back to bite me. "I may have been feeling somehow when I said that," I admit.

"So you did. Love her." The gun gleams black in her hands. "The question is, do you still love her?"

"No." Zero hesitation.

"Are you sure?"

This time my denial is not so quick, but I do say no. And then add, "But I don't wish her dead."

Maggie moves on to the rag and oil. "I think you should go," she finally says.

It's the last thing I expected. "You want me to go?"

"I do."

"Why?" I'm somewhere between shocked and offended.

"You know why."

"Do I?"

Maggie gives me a look.

"If you think I'm still in love with my ex and that's what's keeping me on the couch . . ."

"Then what, Kai?"

"Not that." Maybe it's easier to believe I'm carrying a torch for my ex than to think we've done irreparable harm to each other and no matter how much each of us tries to heal, the wound's still bleeding.

"Then what?" she repeats.

No way I'm answering that, so I change the subject to something less controversial. "What about Grandpa Tah?" Granted, it's a weak protest, but it's not unmerited. "He can't stay here by himself."

"He can stay with Grace," she says. "He loves it at her place, and she could use the extra help getting the grand reopening ready."

A thought occurs to me. Maybe this isn't about healing or next steps. Maybe this is about me being a burden. Maybe me sitting here staring at wallpaper and taking up space in her second favorite chair is tedious, that my inability to move on is a black cloud that Maggie's tired of entertaining. Maybe the simpler truth is that I've overstayed my welcome.

"Are you trying to get rid of me?"

She snaps the revolver back together. Spins the cylinder and it clicks into place. "The last time I let you out of my sight, you joined a cult."

"I knew what I was doing," I lie, but I do it with my whole chest.

She gives me skeptical eyes. "You need to go to the Burque. Maybe for your ex, but mostly for you."

My heart's beating so fast that surely she can hear it. But my tone is casual, unfazed. Maybe a little cold. "If you don't want me here, just tell me to go."

She sets the gun down on the table with a thump and gives me a look of complete exasperation. "I'm not sending you away, Kai. I'm coming with you."

CHAPTER 2

We leave the next morning. Climb into her cherry-red 1972 Chevy 4x4 and head south to Tse Bonito and then east across the checkerboard zone. It's three hours to the Burque. Unlike going west through the Malpaís, the stretch of freeway between Dinétah and the Burque is generally maintained and well-traveled. We don't expect any trouble, but then, who does? Maggie has her arsenal on her just in case, save the lightning sword. (That's gone into the ground out near Wheatfields. Maggie didn't say why, but rumors that someone's been asking about it were enough to part ways with it for now.) I remember the last time I traveled this road—in and out of consciousness after the Urioste goons beat me within an inch of my life—and I find that I don't mind that my kinda-sorta girlfriend is fully armed.

Maggie reiterates what she explained to me at length the night before. I have unfinished business in the Burque and until I face the Uriostes and my past, I won't be able to be fully present in this life . . . or with her. "Maybe you still love your ex—"

"I told you I don't."

"—or maybe you don't. But you won't really know for sure until you see her again. Get your questions answered."

"Like why she threw me under the bus and had me beaten almost to death?"

"Exactly." She takes a sip from her water bottle and offers me one. I decline. She shrugs, slots the bottle into the drink tray, and continues. "I dealt with my past, and it hurt at the time. Sure, it did. But afterward I felt great."

Is she serious? I grab the bottle and swig. "You dealt with your past by binding him and burying him in the ground!" We don't actually know if her old mentor and partner, Neizghani, is dead, and there's been some disturbing rumors that he's been seen in the far Western Agency—another reason to dump the sword—but she definitely trapped him underground with no intention of digging him up.

"Whatever works, Kai." She takes the bottle back.

The truck thumps over something on the road, and I brace myself against the hard bounce. "Besides, I haven't thought about Lala—Lachryma—in months. She's not the problem."

She spares me a glance. "Look me in the eyes and say that."

Fair. Okay. She's not the *only* problem, but I don't think I'm ready to say that to Maggie. "This is you playing therapist, isn't it?"

"I know," she agrees cheerfully. "I've come a long way."

"You're advocating I solve my problems with a gun."

"Ah, so you admit she's a problem."

"Jesus, Mags. I'm not shooting anyone. I told you I don't want her dead. And you know how I feel about violence."

"And that's why I'm coming along."

I stare.

"Not to shoot her." She gives me a look like I'm an idiot. "To protect you so you don't have to get violent. I'll be your bodyguard. But if at any time Lala or any member of her family requires shooting? I'm there for you."

"Thanks." I try for sarcasm, but I'm not sure it lands.

"I won't do anything rash," she continues, confirming she is immune to my disapproval. "But if the opportunity to get a little vengeance on the people who did you wrong presents itself, well . . ."

"I don't need vengeance."

"Sure you do."

"No. I don't."

"Everybody wants revenge against their enemies."

"You might, but I don't. And besides, Lala's not my enemy."

She lifts a dubious eyebrow.

"It wasn't that bad."

"Kai." Her tone is flat.

"I know," I say, raising a hand to stop her from reminding me just how bad it was. When I don't say anything else, she gestures as if to say, *See?*

I scrub my hands through my hair with the vigor of a man defeated. "Questions answered," I say firmly, willing it to be true. "I'm just going to make sure she's not in danger and get some questions answered."

"Unfinished business," she echoes.

If only it was that easy.

I nap for a while after that, the drone of the engine lulling me into a restless sleep. I dream, and it's nothing good. Distorted memories put through a funhouse mirror. I'm in the middle of the Old Town Plaza in the Burque where the Uriostes held my trial and public beating, only this time Maggie's there and she's got a gun. She doesn't shoot me because it's raining, and she doesn't want her bullets to get wet. I tell her it's fine. My wings will keep me dry. She shrugs and points the gun at my heart, but then Lachryma's there and her skin is made of sky-blue paper. She kisses me. At first it's nice. Familiar. But then she won't stop, and she's got my tongue between her teeth and she bites down and my mouth fills with silver blood. I spit, and my tongue falls into my open hand. I look up, and all across the plaza everyone's dead.

I wake with a shout. Bang my head against the passenger-side window.

"You okay?" Maggie asks.

It takes me a moment to remember where I am. That I was dreaming. "Yeah." I press three fingers to my tongue, just to make sure it's still there. "Bad dreams."

"Anything I need to know?"

Probably, but I don't want to explain it all. Don't know if I even can. "I'll let you know if something comes up."

I can tell she wants to argue about it, remind me that dreams are serious business and not to be ignored, especially for a medicine man in training like me. But she can tell I'm rattled, so she lets it go.

"We're coming up Nine Mile Hill," she says, gesturing out the windshield.

"Stop at the top, I want to show you something."

She does as I ask, pulling over to the side of the road as we crest the western edge of the Burque. I climb out and walk around for a better view. Below us stretches the city, cradled in a sun-kissed basin. Almost two hundred square miles along the banks of the Rio Grande, snuggled up against the Sandia Mountains in the east, and held in by indigenous Pueblo communities in the three other directions, a city of pink light and sagebrush cupped in the palm of an unforgiving desert. From up here we can see it all.

"It's exactly how I remember it," I tell her as she joins me, leaning against the still-warm hood. Its sameness is a reminder that I haven't been gone as long as it feels like I have.

"Tell me about it," she says, her voice a reverent hush, like she understands something in this moment of my homecoming is to be respected.

"That's right, you've never been here." I smile, almost nostalgic. From up here it looks almost beautiful. Peaceful.

"Only as a kid. Before the Big Water."

"It was founded in 1706 by Francisco Cuervo y Valdés, the governor of the province Santa Fe de Nuevo México. There were Indigenous people here before the Spanish, of course. Still are. Tanoan and Keresan Pueblo, who pretty much keep to themselves."

"We passed through their lands," she says. "While you were asleep. Walls high as Dinétah's own."

"They've had enough of foreigners and invaders."

"No doubt."

"Apache and Comanche lived here too." I pick up where I left off. "And Diné, of course. All here long before Cuervo y Valdés dedicated this stop along the Camino Real to the tenth Duke of Albuquerque." I point to the line that bisects the city, running north-south. "That's the Rio Grande. It's the lifeblood of the city when it runs, but that's rarer and rarer. Now most of the water comes from catchments in the Sandia Mountains"—I point to the looming mountain range straight ahead of us to the east—"or from the underground aquifer system. All controlled by the Uriostes."

"People shouldn't own water," Maggie grumbles.

"But they do. There's no such thing as public utilities anymore.

You try to collect water without a permit, even rainwater, and that's a good way to get jailed. Or shot."

We sit with the perversion of that for a while.

"What's that?" Maggie gestures toward a mass of air ships and hot-air balloons hovering above the city to the north.

"It's the floating overcity. Abruzzo."

"In the air? It just stays up there? And people live there?" She glances over, clearly dubious. "You ever been there?"

"Once. For a party."

"Unsurprising," she teases, tone dry, but her eyes stay on Abruzzo. "Was there champagne?"

She's never let me forget about telling her about drinking champagne when we first met. But I don't mind. I like that she remembers. "You want to go?"

Her shoulders tighten and she hugs her arms around her chest. "I flew in a plane once. Didn't care for it. Can't imagine a balloon is better."

"Afraid of heights?"

"No." She glares at the offending overcity. "I said I just don't care for them."

"We're going to have to go up the mountain. That's where the Urioste compound is." I nod toward the crest of the eastern mountains where, if you know what you're looking for, you can spot an adobe hacienda on the high summit, jewel-encrusted walls glinting in the setting sun. "We have to take a tram to get there."

"Not a balloon, though?"

"No."

"Then it's fine." She hesitates. "What's a tram?"

"You'll see. But not yet. First, we need to pay a visit to a friend. I don't know if Lala's really in trouble or we're being led into some kind of trap, but I'm not walking into the Uriostes's lair without a little information first."

"Alvaro Cruz?"

I look over, surprised.

Maggie's shoulder comes up in a shrug. "He's the only friend you've ever mentioned, and I know he helped get you to Dinétah. Figured he's a man who gets things done, maybe knows things. Plus, you said his dad was some big shot who worked for the Uriostes."

"Their cacique. You've got a good memory."

"I'm not just a pretty face and a gun."

"No, Mags," I say lightly. "I'm the pretty face."

She laughs, a hint of that rare smile threatening, as she hauls herself to standing and starts back toward the truck door. It's enough to make me brave. "Maggie." I gently grasp her arm. She pauses, looks back. "You don't have to do this. I'll understand if you want to go home." I have to say it. Try one last time to release her from whatever comes next. "You're right that I have unfinished business, but it's not your burden to bear. I can do this alone."

She stares at me long enough for me to feel my face heat and wonder if I said the wrong thing. But finally, she presses her hand to my cheek.

"Yes, I do have to do this," she says. "Because we're partners. Because I love you. And you love me, too. You told me so, once. I haven't forgotten . . . even if you have." She drops her hand and walks back to the driver's side.

I linger, looking over the valley, scared that she's right on all counts.

CHAPTER 3

The sun dips below the horizon, and night falls in earnest as we wind our way down what used to be Interstate 40 and into the Burque proper. What was once an eight-lane highway is now a narrow two-lane road buffered by a makeshift shantytown. The buildings are primarily mobile homes like Maggie's or clusters of those sheds that were popular for outdoor gardening supplies or in-law add-ons before the Big Water. Christmas lights in bright colors run festively across the alleyways between them, running off generators and exterior extension cords. Fires burn in enclosed pits, and the smell of charred meat wafts into the truck cab along with a steady stream of eighties New Wave. It's all pretty festive for the postapocalyptic.

"What's this place?" Maggie asks.

"Little Texas." I motion toward the Texas flag hanging over a tricked-out double-wide. "Mostly Texas climate refugees. New Mexico was always a popular tourist spot for Texans pre-Big Water, so not surprising so many settled here after."

"How big is it?"

"A few square miles here on the city's edge."

She sniffs the fragrant air through the open window. "Smells great."

"Always does. Think what you will about the Lone Star state's former residents, and people definitely have their opinions, but they know their way around a barbeque."

"Where do they get the meat from?"

"I don't ask." I peer into the maze of trailers and tiny houses. "Turn here."

Maggie hooks a right, and we roll down a side road following the sound of some eighties band I can't remember the name of. I hum along a little until it clicks. The Pixies. Already an oldie in her day, but one of my mom's favorites. A memory of her hits me like a sledgehammer. The way she liked to listen to eighties music as she worked at her loom, weaving the same designs passed on to her from her mother and her mother's mother. I can almost hear her telling me to come sit with her, and me complaining that I was too busy playing video games or scrolling on my phone. If I'd known how little time I had left with her, I would have chosen differently. Or at least I like to think I would have. I really don't know. When you're young, it's hard to imagine your parents dying or the world ending. I usually don't let myself think of her, the guilt and grief too immense, but music has a way of unlocking memories, even when unwanted.

"Pull in here." I point to a familiar sign.

Maggie parks the truck beside a red-and-white barn next to a black armor-plated Jeep with *All God's Creatures Vet Care* painted on the door panel.

"Is it a dangerous business, vet care?" she asks, eyes on the vehicle that's more tank than anything.

"People can be aggressive if they think you're carrying drugs. After the Jeep got broken into a few times, Alvaro decided better safe than sorry." I climb out of the passenger's side and look around, more memories bubbling up. But these are good ones. Laughter, friendship, a home away from home. "I used to spend a lot of time here."

"Caring for animals?"

"Sometimes. But mostly playing poker."

A man walks out of the barn leading a horse and chatting with a woman in a baseball cap. He has a mass of curling dark fringe that falls over his spectacled eyes, hair shorn shorter on the sides. His denim shirt is well-worn and a size too big for his frame. He's probably a good two inches shorter than me, but I always think of my best friend as a giant in my memory.

"Watch him for a few days," Alvaro says to the ball-capped woman, "and if he's still not eating, bring him back. And, Kris, you need to take better care of his feet. I'll see what I can do to help you cover expenses if that's the problem, but he needs new shoes."

The woman's face crumbles. "How much will that cost?"

"You know your shit is always good with me," he says with a grin, tapping a sack of horse manure the woman's clearly brought as payment, amused at his own joke. "Makes my garden grow."

She nods, looking relieved. "Okay, Doc."

"Not a doc," he corrects her. "Just a sometimes ranch hand who learned his way around animals who's doing what he can to help."

She nods and gives him a hug before she leads the horse away. He watches her go and then notices us loitering.

"Closing up shop for the night," he calls, lifting a hand to shade his vision from the blinding overhead barn lights. "Unless it's an emergency."

"It's kind of an emergency," I call, stepping forward. "Last time I checked, you still owe me money."

"Kai?" Alvaro's eyes widen and a grin splits his face. He throws his arms wide, and we meet in an embrace. "Jesus, Kai," he mumbles against my neck. "I thought I'd never see you again."

He smells like animal fur, manure, and a faint hint of something medicinal, but I happily breathe it all in before breaking the hug and stepping back.

"Same, my brother," I admit. "Same."

"And look at you! You look great! Who patched you up? Your grandfather?"

"Yeah, my cheii." I shoot Maggie a warning look that I hope she understands. We didn't talk about it beforehand, but I'd rather not mention clan powers to Alvaro. It's a lot to explain, and if I open that can of worms, who knows what else will slither out?

"No limp," he continues, oblivious. "And your face is perfect!"

"I tell him that every day," Maggie says. "I think it's starting to go to his head."

Alvaro takes Maggie in, eyes skimming over the shotgun on her back, the knives and guns. But this is Little Texas. People like their guns, and Maggie doesn't stand out like she would in politer company. But he does notice her classic truck, and nods appreciatively.

"My apologies," Alvaro says. He sketches a bow. "Alvaro Cruz. Sort of veterinarian. At your service."

"Maggie Hoskie," she says, inclining her head. "Monster slayer."

Alvaro's eyes widen. "I've heard stories of Dinétah."

"You don't know the half of it," I say, hand on Alvaro's shoulder as I turn him toward the barn. "Can we talk inside?"

He nods, but his eyes linger on Maggie, who gives him a smile. Not the one I treasure, but the kind that makes a man's insides go to jelly. Alvaro blanches, and I shake my head, bemused. Maybe I treasure that smile too.

"What are you doing here?" Alvaro asks once we're settled indoors. A black dog with a white chest that I don't recognize comes up and sniffs my hand tentatively. She must decide I'm okay because she promptly drops and demands a belly rub. I pop a squat and oblige her because who am I to refuse?

Alvaro has a rotating stable of strays and hard cases of varying species at any given time. There was an orange tabby named Taco in residence for a while that I grew fond of, but I don't see him anywhere. Maybe he's out hunting, but he's just as likely asleep in a pile of hay or under a table somewhere.

Alvaro says, "I wasn't lying when I said I didn't expect to see you again. The Urioste brothers aren't in town, but if they knew you were back in the Burque . . ." He shakes his head. "It's not safe for you here."

I pull the letter from my pocket and hand it to him. He sucks in a breath and gives me a look, no doubt recognizing the sky-blue stationery and the Urioste sigil.

"Read it," I tell him.

He does, and after a moment, exhales a troubled breath.

"Jesus Christ," he murmurs.

"Do you know anything about it?"

He shakes his head and flips the paper over as if maybe the answer is written on the back.

"Do you think it's real?" Maggie asks.

He looks at her, questioning.

"We think it might be a trap," I explain.

"For what? They got their pound of flesh from you, Kai. And Lala's engaged."

I freeze mid belly rub and the black dog whines at my neglect. I give her one last pat before I stand and pace away, trying to digest this news. I can feel Maggie watching me, almost hear her accusation that she was right that I do still have feelings for Lachryma. But that's not it. At least, I don't think it is. I don't know what I'm feeling.

"Who's she marrying?" I ask.

Alvaro doesn't know. "Some rich asshole from New Denver. She and I are still civil, but I haven't really kept up with the details of her life since . . ." He gestures at me.

"Aren't you a rich asshole?" Maggie asks, sounding no more than curious and employing her usual tact. "Kai told me your dad worked for them."

"As their cacique," he acknowledges, looking unfazed by the accusation. "And I like to think I'm not one of the assholes. I chose a different path, and I can't control who my parents are, just what I do with my life."

"And you chose this?" She nods at the barn, at the dog who's moved on to beg pets from her next.

Alvaro pauses, mouth open, as if considering how to answer. "Not entirely," he admits, honesty getting the better of him. "I'd be lying if I said I don't keep some of those connections. But after what they did to Kai, I've kept my distance." He leans forward, arms resting on his knees, pushing back the mass of curls from his face. "It's my fault you got mixed up with the Uriostes," he says to me. "I should never have taken you to that party."

"I wanted to go," I remind him. "And I had a hell of a time."

"Yeah, but—"

"Alvaro. It wasn't your fault. No one's responsible for what happened to me except the Uriostes."

He takes a moment, seems to absorb that. But I can see he's

carrying a lot of guilt. "So why this?" he finally says, waving the letter he's still holding.

"That's what we're here to find out," Maggie says.

"And we want your help," I add.

"Anything," Alvaro says with a sudden burst of real passion. "Of course. Anything, Kai."

And I understand that it's more than just guilt he's carrying. He's looking for a way to be forgiven. He's looking to do penance. And something in my chest tightens uncomfortably because I had no idea Alvaro was suffering because of me. It makes me not want to ask him for help. Not put anything else on him. But the expression on his face—hopeful, determined—tells me that asking for his help is a gift. And if I can help him absolve himself from feeling responsible for my own foolish choices, I'm happy to do that.

"Do you think you can get a message to Lachryma? Ask her to meet? Don't tell her it's me. Give her some excuse."

"Of course," he says, eager. "Tonight?"

"I don't want to put you in any danger."

"It's not a problem." Alvaro checks a clock on the wall. "I do a lot of late-night emergency business. I'll send a runner with a message. Where do you want to meet?"

"The park at the foot of the tram. Eleven o'clock?"

He gives me a knowing look when I mention the park but doesn't argue. Just walks to his desk, retrieves paper and a pencil, and drafts a message. He hits a call button, and a signal goes out on a landline to a messaging service, I presume.

"The runner will come, but it will be a while," he explains.

I nod. And then we all stand around awkwardly for a moment until Maggie says, "Looks like we have a few hours to kill. What now?"

Alvaro opens a bottom desk drawer and startles as an orange cat jumps out. "Dammit, Taco!"

I laugh as Taco yells back at Alvaro, no doubt complaining about his desk incarceration. Alvaro reaches around the offended cat and pulls out a bottle of whiskey and a pack of cards.

"Texas hold 'em?" Maggie asks, eyes lighting up.

"Seems appropriate," Alvaro agrees.

"We playing for trade? No offense, but I'm going to need a little more than a bag of horse shit."

Alvaro snorts, and then looks around, thinking. "I've got some coffee I collected for payment last week. Will that do?"

Maggie rubs her hands together. "Deal me in."

CHAPTER 4

At half past ten we head out, Alvaro two pounds of coffee poorer and Maggie happily humming "People Are People" from the back of the Jeep. After some debate, we decided to stow Maggie's truck in the barn and brave the nighttime streets of the Burque in Alvaro's vet vehicle. Despite the history of break-ins I relayed to Maggie earlier, Alvaro assures us that there's an unspoken rule that people don't mess with All God's Creatures.

"Why Little Texas?" Maggie shouts over the outsized noise of armored-jeep travel.

"My family was originally a ranching family from down near Clovis and the Texas border," Alvaro shouts back as we drive past the abandoned city center and begin the gradual climb up the slope of the eastern mountains toward the neighborhood called The Heights.

"You're a cowboy?"

He tips an imaginary hat. "The real kind. From New Mexico. But Little Texas reminds me of where I grew up."

"And the eighties music?"

At this he shrugs. "It's a Texas thing. I've never understood it, but someone once tried to explain it to me. Something about the Austin music scene in its heyday?"

"Never heard of it."

"It was the capital city," I chime in, voice carrying over the ambient noise. "Long gone in the rising waters."

"The music is good," she says, leaning back. "I like it." She sings along to the chorus. I don't think I've ever heard Maggie sing. If I didn't know it was impossible for Maggie Hoskie to have fun unless she was killing something, I'd swear that's exactly what she was doing.

Alvaro laughs. It's clear he's having fun too, even if Maggie did take all his coffee. "Where'd you meet her?" he asks me.

Maggie's got her eyes closed as she mouths the words to "Blasphemous Rumours."

"She's close to my cheii. He introduced us."

"Are you . . . ?" The implication is clear.

"What if I say it's complicated?"

Alvaro purses his lips. "When is it not complicated with you, Kai?"

"Hey, that's not fair."

"And yet, here you are. Driving out to meet your ex-girlfriend with your *complication* in the back seat."

"I'm very aware that things could get awkward."

"I think you're past awkward. You do remember that Lala almost got you killed?"

"At least she didn't pull the trigger." The words are out of my mouth before I consider the wisdom of them.

Alvaro frowns. "What does that mean?"

I glance back at Maggie and then back to Alvaro. His eyes get big. "You're going to have to explain that one."

"Another time. I promise." But how do I explain what happened on Black Mesa? "You're right. This is probably . . . not smart."

"Very not smart." He looks at Maggie in the rearview mirror. I can tell he has a million questions, and none I want to answer.

"But you're here," I point out. "With me."

"What are friends for?" He laughs at some stray thought. "We've gotten into worse together."

That much is true. I met Alvaro a few years after the Big Water. My dad had already checked out of being a father, too consumed by grief after losing my mom, so I was pretty much on my own. I fell in with a group of street kids, a not uncommon fate in those first few years when so many people were lost or dead and families were shattered. My situation certainly wasn't unique.

But Alvaro was.

Most of us were feral, teenagers prone to risk-taking and screaming at the world to notice us. But Alvaro was different. Quiet, thoughtful, kind. Always along for the ride, but he lacked the death wish that characterized a lot of my other friends at the time. Later on, I would find out that his family was intact, at least in the literal sense. He just chose to run with us orphans. He had explained over a shared bottle of toxic homebrew that his father was a powerful man he had never gotten along with, that Alvaro was expected to follow in his father's footsteps like a dutiful son, but that he had no desire to serve the Familia Antigua. A lot of our mutuals pulled away from him after that, but not me. I appreciated a guy who made his own choices in life. We were different people from different worlds, but we became the best of friends. We had seen each other at our worst and, occasionally, our best. Most people would kill for a friendship like that.

We pull off the main road and Alvaro gives the Jeep a little gas as we climb. The paved road breaks into potholes and then dirt as we reach the crest of a small hill. Now we are deep in the shadows of the mountains, the crescent moon and splattering of stars that had lit the night sky earlier blocked behind the looming cliff face.

We park in the trailhead parking lot at the base of the mountain directly in front of a small sign that says GRAND ENCHANTMENT TRAILHEAD. It's the first place Lachryma and I met after the Fiesta gala, the first place I saw her without a mask on, the first place we kissed. It has some sentimental value to us both, and I hope that's enough to pique her interest. She'll probably wonder why Alvaro picked this place and why he insisted it was vital that she come tonight, especially after he hasn't talked to her for months. No doubt she'll know it has something to do with me, and with the letter burning a hole in my pocket, I hope that knowledge is a good thing. Because now that we're here and seeing her again is imminent, my heart's beating way too fast, and I realize Maggie was right to ask if I still have feelings for her.

"What's the plan?" Maggie asks.

Alvaro clears his throat pointedly, an indication that he wants to speak.

"Go ahead," I say, willing to listen.

"I'll go first," he offers. "Make sure everything's copacetic. Once everything's all clear, you join us, Kai."

"And me?" Maggie asks. Her tone is mild, no more than a questioning, but I can tell she has an opinion.

Alvaro gives Maggie a long look. "How are you with those guns?"

"Extremely good," she says. No more than the truth.

"Yeah, that's what I thought. Maybe you hang back? I don't want to scare Lala away."

"No," I say. "I'm okay with you going first, but Maggie's not staying in the Jeep. She's coming with me."

Alvaro protests, but I don't budge. I know how hard this must be for Maggie despite her willingness to walk this path with me. I won't hurt her any more than I must.

"Would you be okay leaving your weapons in the Jeep?" I ask her.

She seems to think a moment before leaning forward, eyes on me as she rests her arms against the back of the passenger seat. "If you ask me to."

I nod, very aware that her weapons are like her security blanket and her children at the same time. A comfort and the things she loves most, the things that keep her feeling safe in a world that has always tried to harm her. Asking her to leave them behind is no small request.

"I'm asking."

"What if Lala is armed?" she says.

"She won't be," Alvaro assures her.

I don't know that for sure, and I won't lie. "It seems unlikely. She's more of a *hurt you with her money and power than shoot you with a gun* kind of girl."

She studies my face, maybe wondering if I meant something dark with my choice of words. If that's another small indictment of the choices we made on Black Mesa. But eventually she starts disarming.

I turn to Alvaro. "Good?"

He's watching Maggie too, as the pile of knives and guns in his back seat grows. He swallows. Gives me a *you've-got-to-be-shitting-me* look but only says "Sure."

"There." I point to the bobbing light coming down the trail. The three of us watch as a figure with a lantern passes under a flickering streetlight, the overhead glow temporarily exposing a young woman in a black skirt, tall boots, and a blue embroidered coat. It's Lala.

Pale skin, a glowing crown of long dark hair, features like something out of a classical European painting. She lifts her head and looks toward the parking lot where Alvaro's Jeep idles.

"Showtime," Alvaro breathes and opens the door.

Maggie, now free of her guns and knives, clambers into the driver's seat to sit next to me. We watch as Alvaro and Lala meet about fifty feet in front of the truck. She hugs him and they talk, too far away for us to hear them. Alvaro gestures back to the Jeep. Lala squints in our direction and shakes her head, looking confused, and asks Alvaro something.

"She's pretty," Maggie observes.

"Yeah," I agree because she is, and Maggie wouldn't appreciate the lie. "But so are you."

Maggie makes a noncommittal noise. Her expression is lost in the shadows, but I think she smiles. Just a little.

And then Alvaro is motioning to us, and we climb out of the Jeep and walk over to face my past together.

CHAPTER 5

Kai!" Lala cries and steps forward, arms open. I hold up a hand to stop her, making it clear that her touch is not welcome. She freezes, face momentarily slack with surprise, and then she folds away whatever emotion she's feeling and drops her arms. Her expression goes pleasantly blank, very much the princess back in control. She glances at Maggie, obviously curious, but only gives her a small curt smile. And then she turns back to me.

"I'm surprised you came," she says, tone falsely cool.

"You said it was life or death, Lala."

For a moment the ice cracks, and she looks flustered. "I honestly didn't think you would care, Kai. I thought you hated me." Her gaze drops. "And you would have every right to after what my family did to you."

"I don't know how I feel." And that's honest. "But I wouldn't stand by if my inaction meant you were going to die." I exhale, wishing I was a more callous person, one that didn't feel a small flutter in my chest at the familiar scent of her citrus perfume, one that didn't react to the attractive flush of her cheeks. "I don't want you dead."

She takes in my face, the same one that broke under the weight of her brothers' knuckles. And the way I'm standing, totally relaxed, hands in my pockets, when last she saw me both my legs were broken. "I'm glad you're okay," she breathes, her eyes softening. "You look good. Really good. And I like the longer hair." She reaches as if to brush her fingers through it, but must remember I did not welcome her touch, and shifts to tuck her own hair behind her ear instead.

Alvaro coughs. "Tell him what you told me, Lala." He frowns, clearly unhappy. "I didn't know, Kai. I swear. But I said I'd give her a chance to tell her yourself."

Lala wipes her hands along her sides, an unusual sign of nervousness. "It wasn't my idea. At least not at first. But when Mother—"

"Wait. Your mother?" Tiny pinpricks of dread gather at the back of my neck. "Elena is involved?" Of course her mother is involved. Of course she's pulling the strings.

"Let's go, Kai," Maggie says, terse. "This doesn't feel right."

"That's probably a good idea," Alvaro echoes.

Lala looks around at the shadowy trees surrounding us and her voice drops to a whisper. "They're right. Go, Kai. I should have never sent that letter, and you never should have come."

That much is becoming glaringly obvious, but stubborn fool that I am, I plant my feet, feeling childish but mostly outraged. This is a trap, a voice in my head screams, and we should run, far and fast. But I can't leave like this. We still have unfinished business, dammit. And honestly, I need some fucking closure.

"You owe me an explanation. I came all this way. Risked my . . ." I glance at Maggie. "Took a risk. The least you can do is tell me what the hell is going on."

"I'm happy to explain everything," a voice says. We all whirl as Elena Urioste steps from the shadows flanked by a dozen armed guards, guns raised.

Alvaro and I whisper the same expletive at the same time, as Lala shouts with more than a bit of exasperation, "Mother!"

Only Maggie is silent. She steps between me and Elena and drops into a fighting stance. She has her big Böker hunting knife in her hand and I can almost feel the bloodlust wafting off her, her clan power rising in response to the sudden danger.

"I thought you left your weapons in the Jeep," I murmur, words only loud enough for her ears.

"Tried," she answers, voice low. "Promise."

I want nothing more than to kiss her. "Don't apologize, Mags. You're perfect."

Because even though we're outnumbered and Maggie only has a knife when the guards have guns, Elena has stopped her advance and is eyeing Maggie warily.

"Maggie Hoskie," Elena greets her.

"You know my name."

"Meeting you in Knifetown left an impression. I did my research. You have a reputation."

"That's good. Saves the awkward introductions."

Her eyes travel to me. "And Kai Arviso. I see you've recovered."

I don't say anything. My feelings for Lala may be muddled, but my hatred for her mother is crystal clear.

Elena sighs. Pats her hair, which she has bleached ash blond, although there's not a strand out of place. "Well, your reaction is to be expected," she says. "But I mean you no harm." A flat smile, as if she realizes the irony of such a statement. "You see, I've done my research on you as well. Not the boy you were when you left us. But the impressive man you've become since. And I would like very much to have a chat with that new man. I have a mutually beneficial proposal, if you'd like to hear it."

I'm suddenly aware of Maggie humming, low and barely audible, but there. And I know what it is. She's crooning Elena's death song. I only have to say the word. But even if she kills Elena, and I have no doubt she could, I don't think she could take out all of the guards before at least one of them gets a shot off. If I'm hit, it won't be fun, but I'll likely survive. But Maggie doesn't have any special healing powers . . . and Alvaro. I look over at my friend, and he's mad-dog staring at Elena, looking like he'd have my back in a fight just as he has since we were kids, and I know with that guilt riding him, he's likely to do something foolish and get himself killed protecting me. Even if his hands are shaking and there's a fine sheen of sweat at his brow. I could never forgive myself if I got him killed.

"All right, Elena," I say. "You want to talk. I'll talk. But let Maggie and Alvaro leave."

She gestures to her guards, who lower their guns. "They are free to go."

"I'm not leaving you," Maggie says.

"Absolutely not, Kai," Alvaro agrees. "You make terrible decisions on your own."

"Exactly," Maggie says, and the two exchange a knowing look that makes me feel both insulted and incredibly loved.

"Why don't we all go, then?" Elena says, amused. "Retire to somewhere more civilized and break bread together. And you and I, Kai Arviso, will talk."

More civilized required a tram ride up the side of the Sandia Mountains.

"Have you ever ridden in a tram?" Elena asks Maggie as the car lifts off its base and starts the journey up the mountain's sheer rocky face. Elena's sitting across from Maggie and has placed an armed guard on her left and right. She wasn't lying when she said Maggie's reputation precedes her, and Elena obviously isn't taking any chances.

I'm sitting several feet away, three guards between us, Lala next to me and Alvaro facing us on the bench across. It's a big tram car and could probably fit another twenty people, but we're all pressed up along the edge by the windows like cats having to share a carrying crate.

"Can't say I have," Maggie replies. I look for signs that she's nervous about the precipitous climb in a swaying car, but if she is, she's hiding it well. If anything, her eyes keep shifting to her Böker. Elena's claimed it and it rests on the seat next to her. If Maggie wanted to take it back, I'm sure she is fast enough to do it. But for now, and probably for my sake, she seems content to wait.

"This is the longest operable aerial tram in the world," Elena says. "Two point seven miles from base to base."

"Probably not a lot of working trams left in the world," Maggie observes.

"Perhaps," Elena agrees. "Nevertheless, this one was the longest even when there were more. Nothing compares to it. Not in the Alps, the Himalayas." She beams as if she had something personally to do with that feat. "It's going to take us over ten thousand feet up from sea level, and from the top, you will be able to see over eleven thousand square miles."

Maggie's eyes flutter shut. It's hard to read what she's thinking, but she's definitely not interested in Elena's tour-guiding. Elena smooths her hands across the blanket she's placed over her lap. "I owe you an apology, Ms. Hoskie."

Maggie opens her eyes enough to glare in Elena's direction. I lean forward, eager to eavesdrop.

"When we met at Knifetown," Elena continues, "I didn't realize what you were at the time. I thought you were some simple hired gun. My attention was on Clarissa Goodacre when it should have been on you."

"Not really," Maggie drawls, face a mask of unimpressed. "Clarissa's family has a lot of power in Dinétah."

"I do find Dinétah fascinating," Elena says. "The world that has awakened there. Tell me more about clan powers."

Maggie smiles that dark smile. "I'd rather show you."

Elena's eyes widen, and that's the first time I've ever seen the Urioste matriarch look rattled. Her hand goes to Maggie's knife, as if confirming it's still in her possession. Then she clears her throat and looks out the window, cutting the conversation short.

I want to laugh. I doubt Maggie understands what a rare achievement silencing Elena Urioste is, but I'll be sure and tell her later.

Lala touches my knee. "Can we talk?"

Rather than answer her, I take the letter from my pocket and hold it out. She takes it and tucks it in her pocket without reading it. She knows what it says.

"Your mother made you write that, didn't she?"

She glances at Elena who, having come to an impasse with Maggie, is now in conversation with one of the guards. "My mother's methods . . ."

"Are the same as always," I say, theory confirmed. "But you, Lala . . . ? That letter? I didn't expect that from you." But maybe I should have. Maybe Lachryma is more like her mother than I give her credit for.

Her jaw works as if she knows what I'm thinking. "I'm nothing like my mother," she protests firmly, voice low.

"But you sent that letter. You lied."

"I didn't—" She cuts off abruptly. "It doesn't matter. You won't believe me. Why come if you are already set against me?"

Am I being unreasonable? I don't think so. But I take a deep breath and start again. "So your life *is* in danger?"

She shifts in her seat. "Things are complicated."

Aren't they always. "Lala, are you in danger? It's a simple question."

"Did you know I'm getting married?" she asks, flipping a thick lock of her dark hair over her shoulder and looking out the window into the night. "To a man I've never met. Older, very rich. Lives in New Denver and controls the water pipelines coming off the Eastern Slope of the Rockies. Mother wants to secure a water contract and so that's what I am. Due consideration. I'll be his third wife." Her voice wobbles. "He has a reputation, of course." Her mouth twists into a practiced smile.

"What kind of reputation?" I ask, uneasy.

"Oh, you know." There's a tremor in her hands as she folds them in her lap. "After his first two wives died under . . . circumstances, they call him King Henry, as in Henry the Eighth. It remains to be seen if I'm more Jane Seymour or Anne Boleyn."

"Jesus . . ."

She nods once, sharp and tight. "But Mother says we all must make sacrifices."

I take Lala's shaking hands in mine. For a moment, I remember what it felt like to touch her. How it wasn't so bad. How *she* wasn't so bad.

"Lala." I lower my voice. "Will this man hurt you? Is that what you meant in the letter?" Maybe Elena did make her write that letter and maybe it was a manipulation to get me here, but that doesn't mean there's isn't a seed of truth in it.

Elena clears her throat.

Lala blanches and looks up toward her mother. Surely Elena can't hear us. Maybe she just doesn't want us talking at all.

Lala squeezes my fingers. "Is it true that you can do what they say you can do?" she asks is a low whisper.

My pulse spikes, and I'm completely thrown for a second. We've been talking about her, and the sudden shift to talking about me is jarring. "What do they say I can do?" I ask, my sense for danger tingling.

"Never mind." She briefly glances in her mother's direction again. "I shouldn't have said anything."

I shift in my seat and glance at Elena. But she's still talking quietly to one of her guards, not focused on us at all. "Who's talking about me? What are they saying?"

"I think Mother wants to tell you."

"I don't want Elena to tell me," I say, irritated by her evasiveness. "I want you to tell me. I didn't come to the Burque for her. I came for you."

"If it's true, then maybe there's hope. Maybe I won't have to—" She stops herself. "How foolish of me, like a child playing make-believe. Like you're some prince in a fairy tale." She shakes her head. "I've always had my head in the clouds, haven't I? I may have loved you, but you were never a prince."

The insult stings, but the other part . . . She loved me? That feels like a knife in the gut. "Be serious. You never loved me."

Her whole body stiffens. "Of course I did."

"And that's why you threw me to the wolves as soon as your family showed the first sign of disapproval?"

"What choice did I have, Kai?"

"You had a choice. We always have a choice."

"You're saying I should have chosen you over my family? I would have been out on the streets."

"I was on the streets. You could have stayed with me. I mean, if you really loved me." That last part is cruel and completely unfair, but it lands its mark, and Lala flushes hot. I guess even now I want to hear that she would have chosen me.

"And what would we have done, Kai?" she hisses. "Gotten married? Lived happily ever after? We were nineteen. Still teenagers."

She's talking as if it's ancient history, but it was last year. "We would have found a way." Why am I pressing this? Laid out before me, I know she did the sensible thing. And there's absolutely no way I would have been ready for some kind of domestic life.

Her voice is pained. "You don't understand."

The thing is, I do. I understand completely. And I know her situation was impossible. I wish this realization gave me a moment of clarity, offered the closure I want so badly. But it's giving me nothing but more pain.

"I'm just saying you didn't love me." I want her to admit it. Need her to say it, take back that lie. It feels very important.

Her eyes narrow, radiating feelings that are definitely not love right now. "You have no idea what you're talking about."

The tram shudders to a stop. The guards are up and getting us to our feet, two still flanking Maggie. Lala roughly untangles her hand from mine and rushes to join her mother, leaving frost in her wake.

Part of me feel triumphant, proud to earn that cold shoulder, as if that is evidence of her perfidy. But another part just feels like an asshole. I drag my feet and wait for Alvaro to catch up.

He presses a hand against my shoulder. "You okay?"

"Not really," I admit. "Lala's hiding something, but I have no idea what. She's hot and cold and I can't get a read on her."

"So she didn't tell you what Elena wants to talk to you about?"

I shake my head no. "But let's go find out."

CHAPTER 6

It's a short ride in a ten-seater offroad vehicle down a narrow road to the Urioste compound, Elena in the front passenger seat and the rest of us piled into the back with the guards. The compound is a series of houses and auxiliary buildings behind a ten-foot-high adobe wall, all overlooking the Burque. The view is the inverse of the one Maggie and I took in from the top of Nine Mile, seen from the east instead of the west.

Memories flood my mind as we pass through the iron gates and into a wide walled courtyard. Last time I was here it was decorated for Fiesta: tables laden with mounds of hand-rolled tamales and bowls of red pork posole; thick tortillas stacked on plates like layer cakes and delicate fried squash blossoms piled on colorful tableware; legs of smoked meat displayed on jamoneros paired with rare Manchego-style cheeses, the sheep, local, but the process as close as can be imitated for the occasion. Lights had hung from the branches of cottonwoods and wound through yellow chamisa, and a mariachi band had played on a raised bandstand as the Familia Antigua paraded through in their regalia in their version of a Desfile de la

Gente—Spanish kings and queens, conquistadores and princesses decked out in costumes that took the previous year to construct or were passed down from earlier generations. The original Fiesta parade was once in the capital of Santa Fe, but protests by the Indigenous populations drove this celebration of the Spanish reconquest of their lands underground. Now, the holiday is celebrated only in private behind high adobe walls by the people who proudly claim their conquering bloodlines.

Alvaro had invited me that night to my first and only Fiesta. He'd told me it was the best party of the year, a once-in-a-lifetime opportunity to experience the opulence of the Familia Antiqua in all their glory. The fact that it was a masked gala meant that I could sneak in and no one would be the wiser. I remember making a joke, something about a Diné boy infiltrating their ethnostate celebration.

"You're wrong," he told me with unusual heat in his voice. "There's no separating the bloodlines in this place. Indigenous, Spanish, Anglo . . . they all meet here and have for hundreds of years. Fiesta marks a peaceful reintegration, not a battle."

"But I'm not invited." My observation was pointed and implied that I thought he was delusional.

He frowned at that. "Don't be an asshole, Kai. Do you want to go or not?"

Of course I did. And an hour later we found ourselves among the lights and music and feasting, Alvaro dressed as a conquistador with the sigil of some ancient Spanish line his family claimed as a bloodline, and I, in deep midnight-blue velvet, the embodiment of the King of Storms. Alvaro had explained that the King of Storms wasn't so much a person as an event in Spanish lore, and anyway it worked because I'd been studying the weather ways with my cheii, hadn't I? I didn't care enough either way to have an opinion. In truth, I would have worn almost anything to get into that exclusive party.

I spotted Lala almost immediately, dancing with a man I learned later was one of her two brothers, her white ruffled skirts and lace veil gracefully whirling around her. She was a vision, like something out of a fairy tale, pure and perfect and clean. I knew immediately I had to have her. Don't ask me why. Maybe after my conversation with Alvaro, my motivations were dark. Or at least complicated. Part of me no doubt getting some perverse pleasure from the irony of such a conquest. It's an impulse I'm not proud of. Lachryma is a person, after all, not simply a place to plant a flag of historical revenge. But there it was. Needless to say, I came to regret it soon enough. But in that moment? Sweetness.

Alvaro had caught me staring.

"Oh, no, Kai. Not her. Anyone but her."

"Who is she?" If anything, Alvaro's protest made this perfect girl in white more intriguing.

"The untouchable daughter of the most powerful family in the Burque: Lachryma Urioste."

I remember grinning like an idiot. "Challenge accepted."

Alvaro had continued his protests, but I had ceased listening. Lala had already noticed me. I was certainly striking in my midnight velvets and half mask, my blue-black hair rakishly styled in a way I knew was attractive. She beckoned me forward to join her in the next dance. I didn't know the intricate steps, but I quickly caught on, my hand at her waist as I took the lead. We danced most of the night, only stopping to eat and drink and exchange a few soft-spoken words. By the evening's end, we were both smitten. Me, because she really was beautiful and that whole conquest thing was icing on the cake. Her, well, she admitted later that she saw the same sort of challenge in me. I was someone whom her mother would disapprove of and was by no means hard to look at.

What came next were months of clandestine meetings, Alvaro reluctantly serving as our go-between, and one fateful night when we had gotten too careless and she'd snuck me into the family chapel. After a night of passion, we'd fallen asleep wrapped only in a blanket in front of the altar. One of her brothers had come to pray morning vespers and found us. The rest was . . . not a memory I wanted to revisit.

But you see why I protested when she claimed to love me. It was fun until it wasn't. And despite the fairy-tale veneer of our meeting, it wasn't love.

"Did you ever think you'd come back to this place?" Alvaro asks quietly as we pull around a wide stone drive dominated by a sculptured fountain, a mermaid perched atop a marble wave. On Fiesta, clear spring water had gushed from her mouth, but now her lips are dry.

"No," I whisper back. There's a dull ache in my chest. "I never thought I'd see this hacienda again."

"Bad memories?"

"Some . . . but not all." A brush of white lace, the rush of champagne bubbles on my tongue. "It's not that simple." My smile is faint. "My modus operandi, right?"

Alvaro looks at me curiously. "How do you mean?"

I look around to see if anyone's listening to our conversation, but everyone seems lost in their own thoughts. "The path my life has taken." How do I explain? "If I hadn't come to the Fiesta with you, I would have never met Lala, and we would have never been caught. If the Uriostes hadn't done what they did, I would have never gone to my cheii's or met Maggie . . ." I look at her now, a row away, still flanked by armed guards. The opposite of white lace and champagne, nothing like a princess in a fairy tale. But she is here with me, walking this path at my side even though it can't be pleasant for her. I wonder what she thinks of all this, of Alvaro and Lala, of me now that she's seeing this part of my past.

"Good things can come from suffering? Is that what you mean?"

A feeling of déjà vu hits me. I said almost the exact same words to Maggie when I was trying to convince her that clan powers were a gift, not a curse. I'm not sure she ever was convinced. "Yeah, something like that. I wish it was black and white, but it's not."

Alvaro nods, thinking about it. "And sometimes we don't know what's good and what's bad until after it's happened." He shakes his head. "But if I have to get my face smashed in and my legs broken to find out, maybe I'll pass."

"Don't want to do it again," I assure him. But if I hadn't suffered that trauma, my clan powers might never have awoken. And if they had risen at another time due to a different event, they might have taken a different form because my need would have been different. So I have to accept that no matter how painful some parts of my past are, they make me who I am.

"They sure are afraid of your 'complication.' " Alvaro nods toward Maggie as two new guards open the vehicle doors. Maggie steps out under their watchful eyes. Lala goes next, one of them offering her a hand that they didn't offer Maggie. And then Alvaro and I slide forward and follow.

"What do you think Elena's heard about Maggie that has her so spooked?" Alvaro asks as we trail the party inside.

"Can't say." It's evasive but I can't explain Maggie's clan powers without sounding insane. *My sort-of girlfriend possesses a bloodlust that makes her an excellent killer.* "But she's the best at what she does."

"Monster hunting?" Alvaro contemplates that. "Well, Elena *is* a monster."

"Can't argue with that," I say as the monster in question leads us all through an elaborately carved door and into the main house. She pauses in a round foyer, the walls decorated with ornately carved nichos. "Alvaro, Maggie." Elena points to her right. "Down this hallway is a room where you will find food and drink and other refreshments. Lala will escort you. Please make yourselves comfortable while Kai and I have a chat." Her tone is polite but brooks no discussion.

Lala cuts her eyes toward me one last time, but if she's trying to tell me something, I don't know what it is. Then she tugs on Alvaro's sleeve. "Come on." She sounds miserable, and kind of afraid.

"Kai." Maggie gives me a pointed look. "You sure?"

"I'll be okay. If she wanted us dead, she wouldn't have bothered to bring us all the way up here. The park was a perfectly fine place to kill us and dump our bodies."

Maggie looks around at the fine furnishings, the elaborate tiled floors. "Less clean up required at the park. Good point."

"If it makes you feel better," Elena says, sounding amused, "I will leave my guards here. It will be just you and I, Kai. On equal footing."

I'm surprised by the offer. Elena's implied that she knows I have some kind of clan power, which means I'm not helpless. She gives me a look that makes me think that yes, she does know, or at least thinks she knows, and that this is a gesture of trust.

I trust Elena about as far as I can throw her, but I go anyway, and we head back out the way we came.

"Where are we going?" I ask as we cross the courtyard, back past the van and the fountain and toward the chapel I remember all too well. My muscles lock up as if my body recognizes this place as dangerous and knows not to return. I force myself to keep moving.

Elena pulls out an ancient-looking key.

"We don't need to revisit this place," I tell her, a vision of Lala and I in flagrante delicto in front of the altar flashing through my mind. "If you're trying to make a point."

Her expression clouds. "I'm not." She sounds earnest. "This is simply the entrance to the waterworks. Water is sacred, after all." She makes it a pronouncement, but I can't tell if she's mocking me or is dead serious. She fits the iron key in the lock and pushes the door open.

I pause on the threshold, every fiber of my being still protesting.

She turns and looks at me, and her expression is one of complete confidence, the queen moving her pawns into place. I feel small and exposed, like she knows more about me than I know about myself. Like she understands who I am in some fundamental and undesirable way, and my protests are simply my weaknesses writ large.

"Through this door is your past," she says, not unkindly. "But herein also lies your future. I knew Gideon, of course. I met him at one of the Knifetown auctions when he was buying up explosives. He told me about a handsome, charismatic Diné boy he had recently met who had died and lived again. It was not hard for me to put two and two together and determine that the boy might be you. And then when news of Glen Canyon reached my ears, I knew for certain."

"My life is none of your business, Elena." It's unnerving that Elena knew Gideon, knows about my time in the White Locust movement and my actions at Glen Canyon.

"I beg to differ, but that isn't my point. My point is you have a second chance here. It is fate that has brought you back to this place, this chapel, as a different person than you were before. It is a chance to rewrite your life, should you wish." She raises an eyebrow questioningly.

The irony is that I just gave Alvaro that speech about suffering and destiny and not wanting to change the past. But here, with Elena offering me some kind of do-over, damn, it does sound good.

It's not that I don't understand that whatever Elena is going to offer me within these walls will likely be more devil's bargain than saint's blessing, but I want to hear it anyway. I want the choice, the chance to at least consider writing over my painful past. Anyone would, wouldn't they?

She waits patiently until I finally nod. "Lead the way."

CHAPTER 7

Turns out there's a secret trapdoor and staircase under the altar, feet from where Lala and I . . . well, anyway. The entrance opens into a black hole, but when I balk at following her down into the gloom, Elena only laughs. "Don't tell me you're afraid of the dark."

"Not the dark," I tell her with a pointed look.

Me? she mouths, but I can tell my fear pleases her. That's fine. I'm willing to give her that. She's a scary woman and I won't pretend otherwise.

She pulls a flashlight from her pocket and flicks it on. "Better?"

I gesture for her to go first, and she does. A short descent down wooden steps brings us to a platform with a row of metal lockers. Elena withdraws heavy jackets and shoulder bags from a locker and hands me one of each. In each bag is a cannister of supplemental oxygen. She zips up her jacket and hefts her oxygen bag.

"How far down are we going?" I ask, my fear cranking up a notch as the weight of the mountain gathers around me.

"It's only a precaution," she explains, her voice incredibly close in the near darkness. "The high altitude and the abrupt shift in elevation can sometimes be difficult. Don't use them if you don't want to." She flips a switch, and a series of red lights burst to life, revealing a winding staircase that leads deeper into the mountain. My relief is palpable, like lifting a blanket off my head that was suffocating me, but she doesn't tease me again. Despite her bravado, I don't think she likes the dark very much either.

"Careful," she warns. "The way down can be perilous."

We follow the red lights into the bowels of the mountain, the only sound the clank of our footsteps against the steel steps and my nervous breath. I find myself wishing Maggie had come with us. Not to protect me. Despite my admission of fear, I know Elena won't toss me over the side into the abyss or lock me below to rot. She needs something from me, and as long as she does, I'm safe. I just want Maggie here to show her this place. To watch her face as she marvels at this underground world, the massive mountain around us, the growing humidity as we move toward some hidden water source. I want to hear what she would say, the uneasy joke she might crack, the way she would reassure me that no matter what happened next, I wouldn't be alone; she would have my back.

After some interminable amount of time, we stop. We step out onto a platform wide enough for a dozen people to stand on comfortably and I'm grateful for the space even as I feel the chill of an invisible breeze brush my cheek. I pull on the jacket and shove my hands in the pockets, grateful for the warmth.

"We are standing over an underground tributary," Elena says. She holds one hand to her ear and points with the other one. Complete silence falls around us. I strain to hear anything and fail.

"The tributary is a branch of the Santa Fe Group aquifer," she continues. "It provides potable water for the Burque and beyond."

"I thought the Burque's water came from the Rio Grande."

"The dried-up Rio Grande?" she says, her eyebrow arching. "Historically, the water authority diverted water from the Colorado River as it passed under the Continental Divide near the Colorado border. From there it flowed into the Chama River and then into the Rio Grande. But as you may or may not have noticed, the great river runs no more."

"I thought that was your doing."

Her laughter echoes eerily in the darkness. "I'm flattered. But no. My counterparts in Colorado have dammed the Chama's flow and turned the Rio Grande into a boneyard. And the continued drought leaves us nothing to counter their manipulations. Now the Burque survives on only what is left of our groundwater." She gestures widely, taking in the tributary somewhere below us.

She pulls something from her pocket—a small stone that glows white in the crimson-tinged gloom—and motions me over to the railing. With a flourish, she tosses the stone over the side and holds a finger to her lips. Together, we watch the small glowing stone drop into the abyss. Elena's lips move, her voice no more than a breath, as she counts. After some time, she turns to me.

"Did you hear it?"

"I didn't hear anything." And I was listening.

"Right after the Big Water, I could drop a glowstone from the lockers and hit water before I reached five."

It all comes together. "The aquifer is drying up, too."

"More to the point, it's not refilling fast enough. The initial population decimation after the climate flooding slowed the need for potable water, but the Burque has exploded since then. Abruzzo, Little Texas, the refugee communities piling up east of here that stretch from Tijeras to Clines Corners. Did you know my people estimate the population on the east side of the mountain alone will reach a million in five years?" She tilts her head back in exasperation. "Where do they come from? I thought the East Coast drowned. But somehow people keep showing up and *procreating*." She looks back at me. "They will ruin us. The Burque simply cannot sustain them."

I have the urge to point out the irony of a woman who proudly traces her lineage to the Spanish invasion complaining about newcomers but hold my tongue. "I sympathize," I say, "but why tell me? Why show me all this?"

She leans against the railing. "I want you to do what you did at Glen Canyon."

"What exactly do you think I did?" I ask carefully.

Her eyes lock onto mine. "Gideon's plan to flood Dinétah failed because of you. Oh, I know he was insane. But that's hardly a disqualifying characteristic in this world. What he did have was vision. And purpose. And an eye for talent. Until, of course, you betrayed him."

I break her stare and pace away, but there's nowhere to go on this platform hanging in the middle of nowhere, and what felt spacious moments ago now feels claustrophobic. "You make it sound like his plan was reasonable. Like it wouldn't have killed thousands of people, ruined farmland, annihilated structures."

She drops her head for a moment before looking up. "You're right. I'm not arguing that, but what I am proposing will do no such damage. In fact, it will do quite the opposite." A pause. "I want you to refill the basin. Gideon explained the phenomenon of clan powers to me. How the trauma you suffer awakens some ancestral supernatural power, and that yours helps you manipulate elemental forces like rain."

"It's more complicated than that."

"Actually, I think it's very simple." She steps closer, her face mere inches from mine. I can smell the heavy rose in her perfume and under that, the meaty animal smell of her flesh. She is very real, very solid, a force to rival the granite mountains around us.

"Make it rain, Kai," she says softly. "Glen Canyon Dam holds twenty-six million acre-feet of water. How much of that do you think you turned to rain when Gideon blew a hole in that dam?"

"That was different," I say, taking a step back, my hip hitting the railing.

"How much, Kai?" She follows me, relentless, refusing to give me any space.

"Not that. Not millions of acre-feet."

She considers my words. "I will settle for less."

"Elena." She doesn't understand. How do I make her understand? "I can't do what you want me to do."

"I don't see why not." She tosses the words at me like I'm the one being unreasonable.

"I had help."

Her gaze sharpens. "Maggie Hoskie?"

"Yes, but that's not what I mean. I had help from one of the Diné Holy People. A water deity. I could have never controlled that amount of water alone."

"Then start with less. Do it your own way. Take your time." She presses a heavy hand onto my shoulder, her voice urgent in my ear. "I want you to think of all the people in the Burque, all those refugees I mentioned before. What will happen to them when there is no more water? Where will they go? How many will die of thirst? Of diseases? How terrible will their suffering be?"

I bark a laugh. "Don't act like you're doing this out of the goodness of your heart. You benefit from this, too."

"Everyone benefits, even you. Especially you."

"How do I benefit?"

She paces away. "Lala is engaged, but I happen to know she is still very fond of you. It was never her fault that I punished you for your shared transgressions. She argued with me on your behalf. Begged, even. It was quite something."

"She fought for me?" I know that's not important in the scheme of things, but this casual reordering of what I thought to be the truth shocks me almost as much as Lala's earlier declaration of her past love. I always believed Lala turned me over to her family with little hesitation. Even on the tram when she rewrote our history, she never suggested that she had challenged her mother, argued for a different fate.

"Lala's engagement can be broken. After all, we won't need to court that terrible Coloradoan if we have you." She pauses and looks me over like she's thinking of buying me at auction. "I would be willing to welcome you to the family . . . as my son."

"Your . . ." It is the last thing I expected to hear.

I'm sitting, but I don't remember dropping to the bottom step. I fumble for the supplemental oxygen and after clumsily fiddling with the release lever for a second, take a deep, steadying breath in.

"Better?" Elena asks after a few moments.

I set down the oxygen cannister and scrub my hands across my face, wondering how the hell I got myself into this situation.

"Have you discussed this with Lala?" I ask, my voice embarrassingly shaky. As if I'm considering this. As if it's at all reasonable.

"Lala is her own woman. I cannot force her to do anything she does not want to. But I know she would welcome you into her bed, into her life. You would be her savior prince."

"I'm no prince," I protest, an echo of Lala's accusation. It stung when she said it, like I wasn't capable of helping her, but what Elena is saying is that I am the only person who is.

Elena sighs and it sounds like pity. "Think of it. Lala as your wife, the wealth and power of the Urioste name that comes with my daughter's hand. Riches that would ensure you would never want for anything ever again. For the rest of your life. For you and Lala's children and grandchildren."

"I . . ." My thoughts are a jumble as I struggle to process what she's offering me. Everything. Everything I once thought I wanted. I wouldn't be the problematic grandson, I wouldn't be the burden, the useless lump staring at the wallpaper and unable to get out of his own way. I could be the prince in the fairy tale, the hero. Just like that.

"How is your cheii?"

Elena's question jolts me out of my fantasy. "What?"

"He, too, would be taken care of. And you could fund a new facility for Alvaro. Ensure he is able to continue to care for animals in need. And Maggie Hoskie. I don't know what she desires. More weapons? Whatever it is, you could provide it for her. You could provide for them all."

"E-even if I could call the rain . . ." Am I considering this? I'm not considering this. It would be insane. But maybe it's an answer. Alvaro could continue his important work, Tah could live out the rest of his life in comfort. I could probably even help Grace and Ben and everyone else. And Maggie? It would hurt her at first if I left, but she'd move on soon enough. She deserves better than a broken boyfriend afraid of intimacy. "I'm not saying it's possible, but if I found a way, some way . . ."

Her look is long and measured. “Why don’t you think about it, and you can give me your answer after breakfast.”

“Elena—”

She holds up a hand to cut me off and smiles, the curl of her lips ghoulish in the strange reddish light. “Please. Call me Mother.”

CHAPTER 8

The journey back to the surface feels faster than the way down. We dump our jackets and oxygen bags and are back in the chapel in what feels like minutes . . . and Lala is there at the altar waiting for us.

She looks to her mother expectantly and Elena gives her a short, sharp nod.

"Oh Kai!" Lala rushes forward to throw her arms around my neck. I stagger under her affection, but she only laughs.

"I knew you'd come through!" she gushes. "I just knew you wouldn't let me marry that awful man."

This is the same girl who only a few hours ago was claiming that I was no prince? It's enough to give me whiplash. But I don't really have time to ask her about it before she's taken my hand and dragged me to a pew where she's laid out an assortment of charts and notebooks.

"We weren't sure what you would need," Lala says, "so I tried to find everything I could think of. There are the most recent weather forecasts for the region, hydrology reports, topography maps, storm charts, and metrics on the aquifer and the tributary that runs below us. Also, metrics on the Rio Grande and the Chama River, including average rainfall, flow, current depth, etcetera." She flushes. "Do you think it's enough?"

"Lala . . ." I'm feeling dizzy, and not just from the atmospheric changes. "This is all happening so fast."

"It must feel that way," she admits. "But to me, it feels like I've been waiting forever." And with that she leans in and kisses me. Not lightly or chastely, but full on, mouth open and hungry. I'm so shocked that I allow it to go on for a long minute before I can untangle myself from Lala's sudden passion.

Elena clears her throat, suppressing a small chuckle. "Well, perhaps I should let you two work."

"Wait," I call to Elena as she reaches for the chapel door. "I should talk to Maggie."

"Oh." She bites at her lip and checks her watch. "It's so late. Why don't you let Maggie sleep? You and Lala can get reacquainted, maybe even look over some of those weather forecasts." She winks like she knows we'll be busy doing something else, and I can't believe this is the same woman who last year wanted me dead for dating her daughter. "You can talk to Maggie over breakfast."

Lala tugs on my arm, and I gently but forcefully push her off. "We'll be working," I say firmly, for both her and her mother's sake.

"You're to be husband and wife now, Kai," Elena says. "It's none of my business." Another little chuckle, and I want to tell her that she has the wrong idea, but I'm suddenly not sure what the right idea is. I didn't agree to marry Lala down there. I said maybe. Maybe. Why does it feel like these two women have decided that means yes?

"Sorry," Lala says sheepishly as Elena leaves. "I didn't mean to make you uncomfortable."

"It's fine." I wipe my mouth, the feel of her lips against mine lingering. And the kiss wasn't bad, but all I can think of is Maggie. How *her* lips feel, how *her* hips feel pressed against mine, the warmth of *her* skin when she's wrapped in my arms. And with a sudden sharp ache, it's all that I want.

"I think I should go check on Maggie."

"Kai," Lala says with a touch of exasperation. "Let the poor woman sleep. It's three a.m."

"Is it?" I had no idea we were underground so long. "Time felt different down there."

With a patient smile, Lala reaches past the collection of notebooks and charts and retrieves a picnic basket. "I brought food. Sandwiches and coffee." She unscrews the lip of a thermos and pours me a cup. The scent of coffee fills the room, warm and earthy, but all it does is remind me of Maggie, and the ache I have to touch her, the desire to see her face, becomes even more acute. But Lala has a good point. I did drag Maggie out here, and the news I have to share with her is not going to be welcomed. So maybe I should let her sleep for a while.

"Here," she says as she hands me the cup. "Let's work a bit." She holds up her hands in innocence. "And I'll keep my hands to myself, if that's what you want."

"Yeah." I tear at my hair, thinking that never did I think I'd be turning down Lala's touch, but I am. I take a sip of coffee. "Let's just work."

We've finished the thermos of coffee and demolished half the food in Lala's picnic basket when I push back from the makeshift desk strewn with meteorological reports and the topography charts of northern New Mexico.

She smiles wanly and stifles a yawn. "Well?"

"I don't know," I admit, rubbing at my eyes, which feel heavy despite the amount of coffee I've consumed. "These reports suggest there's a lot of moisture in the upper atmosphere moving down off the Eastern Slope, but I'm not sure how I would keep it from evaporating before it reached the surface. I'd have to cool the air. I've never done anything like that before, but technically it could be done. I'm just not sure how." Damn, I'm so tired my eyes are starting to cross. "This is . . . really different."

She reaches over and pats my leg in sympathy. "You'll figure it out. You're just stressed." She motions for me to turn around. "Let me help."

I turn warily, not sure what she's up to, but she only massages my shoulders. I exhale as she works the muscles in my neck and upper back.

"Good, right?"

I grunt a sound that passes for yes. She continues for a while until I can feel the tension lessening and my eyes droop closed, and suddenly, I could sleep right here and now, stretched out on this wooden pew with nothing but a pile of charts for a pillow.

"What time is it?" I ask. There are no clocks in the chapel, and I don't have a watch. There aren't even any windows to monitor the sunrise.

"Not sure."

"I should really go check on Maggie," I say around a yawn. "I don't want her to wake up and not know where I am."

And I've put off the inevitable long enough. Time to man up and face whatever comes next.

Lala's hands still. "Kai . . ."

"I don't even know if she slept," I babble on, eyes still closed, a small smile at the thought of seeing Maggie again lifting my lips. "Sometimes she stays up all night, cleaning her weapons or chatting with my cheii. It's silly because it hasn't been that long, but I miss her. I'm sorry, Lala, but it's the truth. I didn't realize how much until now."

She's silent behind me and I know I've probably said too much, but the long day is finally catching up with me.

"I'll do what I can to help here," I say, "and while I don't trust your mother or your family to do the right thing, Elena's not lying about the water. The Burque needs water. But I don't think I can stay. What your mother offered me is . . . well, it's amazing. And you're great. But you're not Maggie." And it's so obvious now that I've said it, now that I've admitted it to myself. How did I ever think otherwise? "And I have a family. I mean, not a mother, but, and no offense, Elena's not my first pick. Or my second. In fact, Grace Goodacre's not so bad if I really need a mother figure. And I have a family, not just my cheii, but everyone back at the All-American. Grace, but Rissa and Clive, too. Even Caleb." I grin sleepily. "Definitely Ben. So yeah . . ." I trail off as I realize her hands are gone and she's dead silent. Of course she is. I just rejected her. Rejected everything. She's probably very, very pissed.

I turn around and she's sitting, head down and hands folded in her lap. Not mad. More . . . worried.

And suddenly I'm wide awake.

"What is it?" I ask, a sudden tightness in my chest.

"Maggie's gone, Kai," Lala whispers.

The tightness in my chest becomes an unbearable vice. "What do you mean?"

"Alvaro took her home. Right after you and Mom when down into the aquifer."

"But Elena said . . ." God, when has Elena ever told the truth when she could lie instead? But Maggie . . . "Maggie would never leave without me."

"She would if I told her we were getting back together."

"Did you?"

"I could have."

"She wouldn't believe you."

She looks up, eyes with a bit of steel in them. "But you did pick me. When you came out of that cavern, you said yes. You kissed me."

"*You* kissed *me*," I protest. "And I told your mother maybe. Maybe. And now I'm saying no."

She stands up and paces away. "Well, it doesn't matter. It's too late."

"It's not too late." My voice rises in irritation. "I'll just go back on the tram. Catch a ride back to Alvaro's or something." I have no idea who to call or how I'll do that, but that doesn't matter. I can walk to Little Texas if I have to.

"No, I mean it's too late. Maggie's gone."

That vice crushing my chest becomes a feeling of vertigo, like I'm standing on the edge of the cliffs of the Sandias looking out over the city, nothing between me and a drop of thousands of feet.

My words come slowly, part panic and part growing rage. "Where. Is. She. Lala?"

"Mom knew she was dangerous, that she wouldn't go peacefully. She has a reputation, like she said. And powers. Not like yours with the weather, but worse. Violent."

"What did Elena do?"

"Alvaro's a vet and he had some drug . . . etorphil or etorphant . . . ?"

"Etorphine." I remember Alvaro using it when he had to put large animals under. I also remember him warning me that it was very potent and very lethal to humans.

"Etorphine," she confirms.

"Alvaro wouldn't do that," I say, but then I think of his father and his connections to the Familia Antigua. Maybe he felt like he didn't have a choice. Maybe he's trapped under Elena's thumb, and I failed to see it.

"But he did," she says sadly. "She had him slip some in her drink."

"The whiskey? But that was before you even knew we were coming." Was Alvaro in on this all along? Was all his concern, his guilt, a ruse? I can't believe it. He's one of the best people I know. But what Lala is saying makes a horrible kind of sense.

"I don't know the details," Lala says. "Tea, I think. Or maybe even coffee?"

A shudder runs through my body. My gaze flickers to the empty thermos, but Lala shakes her head. "No, of course not. I drank that coffee too. And Alvaro gave Maggie just enough to knock her out so she wouldn't fight when she realized you weren't going back with her."

But that doesn't make sense. Lala may think once Maggie wakes up in Little Texas, she'll calmly accept defeat, tuck tail, and run home. But she doesn't know the woman who tracked me all the way across the Malpaís, who saw me sit at Gideon's right hand and still didn't give up on me.

But Elena. Elena would know. She would know that as soon as Maggie woke up, she would never believe I had willingly stayed, and she would know that Maggie would come for me, raining down hell on the way. And Elena would make sure that never happened.

"I've got to go!" The surety that Maggie's life is in danger is a bolt of panic that cuts through everything. I run to the chapel door, but when I wrench at the knob, it doesn't turn. I do it again, hard, but it refuses to budge.

I turn to see Lala cowering in the corner. "Give me the key, Lala."

"I don't have one," she squeaks. "It locks from the outside."

"Fucking open the door, Lachryma."

"I can't!" she yells, sounding desperate. "It's too late, Kai. Don't you see? Mother's done what she does, and you just need to accept it. It's not so bad. *I'm* not so bad. Don't you want me?"

I rally as much contempt as I can and sneer, "You're nothing like Maggie." She flinches, and I'm glad it hit the mark. She may not be quite the monster that her mother is, but she's been lying, too. Manipulating my emotions, my guilt, my confusion. Taking advantage of my feelings for her, my desire to do the right thing. And if she had anything to do with hurting Maggie, I swear . . .

I bang my fist against the door and rattle the knob again. "Hey!" I shout. "Let me the hell out! Someone open the damn door!"

I hear a distinctive click, one I've become very familiar with over these past months. And sure enough, I turn to find Lala pointing a gun at my chest. But her hands shake, and her grip lacks confidence. It's clear she's never shot someone before.

Which would be funny, except it's not. But I find myself laughing anyway, as I say, "I've been shot by better women than you."

She blinks, taken aback, but in that moment of threat, I can feel my clan powers rising, the sudden confidence that I could talk the sun into refusing to rise and the moon into hiding her shine if only I asked.

"Put down the gun, Lala," I say, and it's not just me, but Kai Silvertongue speaking, Bit'aa'nii whispering.

Lala drops the gun immediately.

"Take three big steps away and face the wall," I say, and she does. I once told Maggie that I couldn't convince anyone to do anything they didn't want to do. Mine was more a power of suggestion than conversion. That fact is the only thing that keeps me from throttling Lala where she stands. Her easy compliance means she likely didn't want any of this to happen the way it has. That she's probably just as much a pawn in her mother's games as everyone else. That doesn't mean I forgive her, but it does count for something.

One last command: "Stay there until I leave and then count to a thousand." I don't know if she'll do it. My "suggestions" are usually not that specific. But she doesn't tell me no. She just starts at one.

I retrieve the gun and tuck it into my waistband at the small of my back. Then think twice and take it over to the door. I'm not familiar with guns. Never even shot one, and I made a small case out of refusing to carry one when Maggie wanted me to. If she were here right now, she'd give me shit, probably gloat a little, and I would deserve it. I channel some of that energy, point the gun at the lock, and pull the trigger.

The recoil throws my arm back and I curse, but after another shot, the lock gives. I kick the mechanism hard, and the door flies open. I step into the courtyard, blinking at the light. It's not just daytime, it's probably close to noon. The sky is a scattering of cumulus clouds, and the sun is high and hot above the mountains.

The gunshots must have been heard in the house because a handful of guards are pouring out of a nearby structure, and Elena joins them from the main hacienda. I think about pointing the gun at her, but I'm no Maggie. Shooting a door at point-blank range is one thing—even I couldn't miss that. Elena and a dozen armed guards who are already pointing their rifles at me make my choice clear.

I drop the gun and hold up my hands.

"What's going on?" Elena demands, and then her eyes widen as she notices the gun. "Where's Lala?"

"Inside." Then I add, "Unharmed. Can you say the same for Maggie?"

And there's a deep well of grief threatening to drown me, a living monster just waiting for me to look in its direction and be devoured. But I won't. I can't. I can't believe that Maggie . . . that anything bad has happened to Maggie. It's impossible. She's too tough, too smart, too incredible for even someone as selfish and evil as Elena to touch her.

Elena lifts her chin, defiance glinting in her eyes. "She was a distraction, Kai. I could tell she was holding you back."

"I agreed to help you!"

"For now," she acknowledges. "But next month, next year? Even when I offered you the world, you had doubts. What else would make you hesitate besides some misguided feelings for that woman?"

Misguided feelings? No. Maggie deserves more than that.

"Love."

She lifts an eyebrow, clearly dubious. And I take a step toward her.

I feel the guards tense, their hands flex, their fingers nervous against triggers. But I've been shot before and survived. Yes, survived. So what am I doing wallowing in sorrow? Why am I obsessing over death when I'm very much alive? Elena was right. I've been given a second chance, and I may never understand why. But maybe I don't need to know. Because all I really need to do is to use the time I have to care for the people I love, and one of those sure as shit is Maggie Hoskie.

"It's love," I repeat. "I love her. And I'm such a fool that I was too scared to admit it. Too worried about getting hurt, about hurting her. But I'm not scared anymore, Elena. You've freed me from that, freed me from the past. So maybe I should thank you. But you should know that if you have hurt the woman I love, if she so much as has a headache from the drugs you forced Alvaro to give her, I will tear you limb from limb."

She scoffs, but I can tell my words have surprised her. "Do your worst."

And so I do.

It starts as a whisper, words barely audible as they leave my lips. But slowly I let the sound grow, speak words to match my desires, my *rage* at what Elena did to me in the past, has tried to do to me again. And did to someone I love.

And when my words and my intentions have become so powerful that I can't hold them back, I scream them. The words hit the air like a deluge. Not as a suggestion, but as a command. They demand, they require, they compel the elements to do as I say, to bow to *me* . . . and Elena gags. And then she gags again, hands clutching at her throat.

I watch as she fights to breathe. She's not worried yet, just confused. But then the slightest bit of panic sets in. I can see it in her eyes, in the way she tries more and more desperately to clear her throat, and finally in the horror that crosses her features when she coughs up an ocean of bile.

I scream the words again.

And she's on her knees, and she's drowning, gagging as the fluids in her body bubble to her lips, and her limbs begin to wither, and her skin tightens as all the moisture in her body gathers in her throat, soaks her lungs, and blocks the air she needs to keep her alive.

I go to her then. Bend down beside her where she struggles on all fours.

"You wanted me to call the waters," I whisper, voice as cold as the cooled air now swirling around us. "And so I have."

She can't answer me. She just looks up, eyes bulging, face distorted, skin desiccating.

"You should have never touched the woman I love."

Those are the last words Elena Urioste hears before she topples over dead.

CHAPTER 9

Three things happen next.

I fall to my knees and vomit up the sandwiches and coffee I consumed earlier.

I feel something wet against my skin and realize it's raining.

And Lachryma Urioste calls my name: "Kai?"

I'm too busy being sick to reply, but when my nausea has run its course, I make the mistake of looking at Elena's desiccated corpse, and the heaving starts all over again. Even worse, I realize that her guards are dead, too. All drowned in the same way, by their body's fluids. I didn't mean to hurt them. My wrath was for Elena only.

"I've got to get to Maggie," I mutter. I did this for her. I killed for her. I'd never killed anyone before, never even done more than throw a few punches in middle school. I'm Kai Arviso and I could talk my way out of any problem. I've never needed violence when I had words.

But now my words and my will have killed. And besides sick to my stomach, I'm not sure how to feel. I'm mostly numb. In shock. Maybe if there had been blood and guts, I would be reacting differently. But the mummified corpses make the violence feel distant and not quite my own.

"Kai," Lachryma repeats, voice shaking, "what happened?"

I lift my face to steadily increasing rain and let it wash my face. I wish I could take a moment to celebrate that it worked, that I called the rain, but it seems peripheral now. A by-product of my rage, not the nurturing miracle that it is. As if in acknowledgment of that truth, thunder cracks across the sky and the clouds that have gathered above in a thick black mass open up in earnest, the precipitation not rain but sharp, icy spikes pebbling the ground in tiny white balls.

"Kai, say something! I . . . what *happened*? What . . ." She breaks off in a hysterical sob.

I did this, and as much as I want nothing to do with Lachryma right now, as much as I just want to find Maggie and makes sure she's okay, I have to stay here and face what I've done.

I push myself to my feet. Lala's crumpled in the chapel doorway, hands over her mouth, eyes wide and terrified.

"I'm sorry, Lachryma." God, how fucking inadequate, but it's all I have. And I reach for something else to say. Something good. "But you're free now, and maybe you don't have to be a monster like her. Maybe you can be someone different. Someone better."

She stares like I've lost my mind, not understanding. And I realize she has no idea that I'm the cause of all this death. I'm harmless, right? The boy who was beaten in the Old Town Plaza, whose special power is making it rain. And it's a long leap between weather ways and what has happened to her mother, too far for her mind to make the connection.

"If this rain keeps up then the basin should fill," I tell her, looking out over the city, "but so will the Rio Grande. The storm I have called is a big one, I can tell. All that high atmospheric moisture coaxed low to the earth. The river won't run forever, but it will give people a chance to fill their tanks, hoard some for the future." I look at her, some of my earlier disgust surfacing past my horror. "Nobody should own the water."

She just stares at me, her dark hair drenched and sticking to her face and neck, the lace on her skirt wilting. She's in shock, but I have nothing else to say to her.

"I've got to go now," I tell her, retrieving the gun that I dropped. "I need to find Maggie."

But taking one of the vans and driving back to the tram won't work. Even if there was someone there to operate the tram and willing to take me down the mountain, it would take too long. I can't leave Maggie out there by herself, maybe hurt or worse.

So, in my moment of need, I turn to my clan powers one more time.

I'd done it before at Glen Canyon and it feels so natural now, so normal when it should be impossible. I call the wind. And it swirls around me, lifting me off the ground. I spread my arms for balance, fight the sudden vertigo of being airborne, and ask the wind to take me down the mountain.

It sweeps me off the sheer face of the cliff and down the mountainside, hurtling me toward Little Texas.

CHAPTER 10

I register Maggie's truck still parked in front of Alvaro's clinic and his armored Jeep right next to it before I'm through the door shouting, Lala's gun in my hand.

"Kai?" Alvaro stands at the kitchen sink, frozen in the act of scrubbing a pot.

"Where's Maggie?" My voice is as icy as the patter of hail against the rooftop. And I've got the gun pointed at the man I consider my best friend.

"Put the gun down," he says, voice steady. The voice he uses on a particularly spooked and dangerous animal.

"I've never shot anyone," I tell him. "And to be honest, I'm probably a terrible shot. But I just killed Elena and her guards so if I miss, I will find a way to kill you. I can promise you that."

"You did what?" comes a familiar voice from behind me, and I whirl in surprise.

Maggie's standing there, Taco the cat in her arms, looking mildly scandalized. "I'm not much of a cat person," she says with a shrug, "but this orange guy kind of grows on you."

"You're alive," I breathe, and I realize I didn't know if I believed she would be until this very minute. And the fear, the abject fear that I've avoided facing, melts away on a wave of emotion so strong I feel myself tearing up.

"Yeah . . ." She nods pointedly at the gun in my hand, and I immediately set it down on the table, something like embarrassment heating my face at the way I barged into Alvaro's like some kind of asshole John Wayne. "But did I just hear you say that Elena isn't?"

"Lala said she drugged you. Or had Alvaro drug you." I look over at my friend who's turned the tap off and is looking at me like he's never seen this side of me before and isn't sure if he should be impressed or terrified. "Etorphine."

"Elena told me to," Alvaro admits. "But I didn't."

"But your father?"

He lifts a shoulder. "My dad can take care of himself. He always has. I told Maggie what Elena had planned, and she played along."

"Wasn't hard," Maggie adds, running a hand across Taco's head. "Just act drunk and headed for dead. Let Alvaro drag me out of there."

My relief at finding Maggie alive is turning to mild outrage. "And were you going to tell me? Or was the idea to leave me up there wrapped in Elena's clutches and married to Lala?"

Taco mews, and Maggie lets the cat leap from her arms to stalk over to his food bowl.

"That was still your choice, Kai," she says to me, eyes level.

"Maggie was never in danger," Alvaro adds, "but she wanted to let you decide between her and Lala without interference."

"Elena offered me everything I thought I wanted. Not just Lala. But wealth, status, a perfect future and a family." I take a step toward Maggie. "But I realized I already have everything I need."

I'm standing before her now. She is waiting, arms crossed, and I reach out a hand. After a long look, she takes it.

"I'm sorry it took the thought of losing you to get through my thick head," I whisper, relishing the weight of her hand in mine, the way our fingers intertwine. "But I love you, Maggie. And I don't care anymore about the past. I want this, I want a future with you."

Her expression cracks just a little. "Took you long enough to remember."

"Can you forgive me?"

Her eyes narrow playfully, and she nods. And then she's in my arms, and my mouth is on hers, and it's the best fucking feeling in the world as my hands slide around her waist and pull her tight.

"Jesus, get a room," Alvaro mutters from somewhere behind us.

"We're taking yours," I say as I lift Maggie up.

"I'd leave if I were you," Maggie adds as she wraps her legs around me, and we stumble into Alvaro's bedroom. "And take a raincoat!" I hear him mumbling complaints and the front door slam.

"That is you making it rain, isn't it?" she asks.

"Yeah." I kick the bedroom door closed.

"I'm impressed."

"I'm about to impress you more," I murmur between kisses as she pulls me onto the bed and her hands are on my belt, and mine are tugging her shirt off over her head. And I can't stop touching her, tasting her. Her mouth, her neck, her breasts. As I work my way down her belly, she says, "You're going to have to tell me what happened up on the mountain."

"Mmmhmmm . . ." I slide off her pants.

"And how you pointed a gun at Alvaro when I couldn't even get you to hold a gun when we were fighting monsters."

"Hmmmm . . ." I let my hands and tongue explore the soft wetness between her legs.

"And . . . oh shit, Kai." She moans and it's the sweetest sound I've ever heard. She presses her hands against my head, and I make her moan again. "And we're definitely going to talk about killing monsters," she says breathily, "because that's not your job, Kai, that's my job, and I don't want you going and getting your hands dirty when you're supposed to heal people and ohhhh . . ."

Her fingers tighten as she grips my hair. I pause, lifting on one elbow. "I promise I am not trying to take your job, Mags, and we can talk about whatever you want tomorrow. But I'm going to need you to focus right now on how much I love you. Do you think you can do that?"

She giggles. Yes, Maggie Hoskie giggles, and blesses me with that smile that's worth living for. "Does this mean you're not sleeping on the couch anymore?"

"That's exactly what this means."

"Good," she says as she pulls me up, flips me on my back, and straddles my hips. "Because that shit was getting old, and I've been wanting to do this for a long time."

She starts to move against me, and it's all I can do not to cry out.

"I love you, Kai Arviso."

"I love you too, Maggie Hoskie."

"We're going to be okay."

"Yeah," I agree. "I think we're going to be just fine."

The End

ACKNOWLEDGMENTS

This is a short story collection, so I'll keep it short.

Thanks to all the editors and publications that first accepted these short stories in their various forms. No doubt many felt questionable (cowboy vampires) or simply unexpected (Black lesbians in 1880s New Mexico), but you rolled with it, and I am eternally grateful.

Thanks to Joe Monti and the crew at Saga Press, and thanks to my agent, Sara Megibow.

Thanks to my husband, Michael, and my daughter, Maya, who was ten years old when I published the first story in this collection and is now eighteen and soon off to college.

And lastly, thanks to you, the reader. Couldn't have done it without you.